A Life in Tales

by
David Roberts

Sometimes not having a story is *the story.*

"There There" Tommy Orange

Copyright © 2024 David Roberts

ISBN: 978-1-917129-76-3

All rights reserved, including the right to reproduce this book, or portions thereof in any form. No part of this text may be reproduced, transmitted, downloaded, decompiled, reverse engineered, or stored, in any form or introduced into any information storage and retrieval system, in any form or by any means, whether electronic or mechanical without the express written permission of the author.

For JABS

This book was made especially for you

Time now to make your own stories

Foreword

Here are some of the remarkable people, places and events that have shaped my life. What you have in your hands is not a life story. Rather, these short stories describe episodes from my life. But they are also moments from the lives of others. In some stories the main character is another though in each, I am somewhere in the shadows. I hope that a sense of me emerges clearly over the collection. What is that person like? That is best for the reader to judge. My wife Nadia describes me as a romantic. Guilty as charged.

She is prominent or proximal in most of these short stories. As will become apparent, many of these events could not have happened without her. Furthermore, but for her encouragement and belief in me as well as her tolerance, the tales would never have been written. For these gifts, I owe her a huge debt as I do for so much else, not least our two beautiful daughters.

The events described in this volume are true insofar as my memory can be trusted. Where detail might have been tweaked for effect, the essence is sound. One exception is in "The Piano" where artistic license has been invoked for the denouement. Some names and locations have been altered in an attempt to protect individuals where it is deemed necessary.

Contents

A Bunch of Keys 1
The Chaplain 4
The Beginning 11
Homecoming 18
Comrade Secretary 26
Fathers and Daughters 32
The English Girl 37
Nostalgia 49
The Bear 55
Light Show in Addis 66
Death in Harar 74
A Patch Of Grass 79
Afrikaners 87
Macbeth on the Mountain 92
Jewels and Binoculars 99
Did You Say Something? 106
The Power of Song 110
The Piano 114

A Bunch of Keys

Comfortable to hold with the heft of a quarter pound bag of toffees, the bunch of keys, in any other thirteen-year-old boy's hand would be the perfect weapon, ready to hurl at the unsuspecting wagtail before it had a chance. In his hand, though, it presented little threat. He was a very weak thrower.

Returning the ball was only one of the cricket skills in which he was sadly lacking. He was no better at catching, batting or bowling, much to the irritation of his housemaster. The only time that the compulsory cricket afternoons were comfortable was when he could recline on the grass during his team's innings. He knew he would not be called upon so he had time to lie on his back on the grass, stare at the sky and blow the clouds away from the sun.

"Anything can be replaced nowadays," the housemaster had declared on numerous occasions. "With the wonders of modern medicine, you can get a new part, including an eye so there is no reason to be afraid of playing cricket."

The boy was never able to unsee the first X1 wicketkeeper having his teeth sprayed from his face. He had missed the flight of a viciously quick delivery by his best friend, the team's opening fast bowler.

But cricket wasn't his main fear. The housemaster did not seem to realize that the boy was more afraid of him than he was of struggling to play the game. He had caned him twice on the backside for talking back to the house matron. He was also embarrassed to be selected on the new housemaster's first day to take his baby for a walk in her pram whilst the other lads looked on in derision. The master was fond of rapping boys across the knuckles with the edge of a wooden ruler for crimes like whispering in class. The boy felt strongly that there was no way in which he could please the master and in fact he felt picked on. This feeling of victimization fuelled his fear. Now he was holding the housemaster's bunch of keys whilst staring at the bird.

He had been asked to leave the classroom and return to the boarding house to collect the master's keys from his wife. The road from the classroom block to the boarding house and the housemaster's flat was only a few hundred yards. Though he was nervous should anything go wrong, he was delighted to have been able to escape the classroom and get outside for this unexpected excursion into the spring sunshine. He hadn't been away from class long and nothing had gone wrong; this was just his irrational fear. The master's wife had handed him the hefty bunch of keys and here he was, on his way back to the classroom. He dawdled, enjoying the spring sunshine, wondering whether this pleasant errand might indicate a slight change in the housemaster's attitude towards him. He allowed himself time to take in the surroundings. On his right was the magnificent neo-classical architecture of the main school block with its two hundred feet central clock-tower. He admired the acres of playing fields rolling down to the banks of the River Stour to his left. It was said that some unhappy boarders had attempted to escape by swimming across. This brief period of solitary liberty lifted his usual deep misery and for a while he felt happy.

Then he saw the bird. The wagtail stood on the kerbside, not fifteen feet away when he first spotted it. He stopped still, both to admire the bird and to steal a few extra minutes from History with his housemaster. It was a rare treat to have any reason to get out of class so this one was not to be rushed. He took delight in watching the little tail bobbing mechanically up and down. It was such a pleasure to enjoy the bird and to take a rare unstressed instant to take in the view across the vast playing fields to the distant River Stour.

He admired the little wagtail. It was minding its own business in the spring sun, pecking at the grass near the kerb unaware of the potential danger it was in being confronted with a teenage boy hefting a weapon. Any other boy would have thrown without thinking though the likelihood is that the bird would have flown away in time anyway. Not this boy though. Lacking confidence in his aim as well as having compassion for the bird, he hesitated. This hesitation was fortunate as it was then that he spotted the drain. There were three or four rainwater drain covers along the edge of the road and the wagtail was bobbing on the roadside beside one of them.

Relief washed over the boy as he pocketed the keys. The bird did not have to suffer and he had good reason not to chance his arm. He would probably have thrown well wide any way but there was the awful possibility that the keys might have fallen into the drain and he would have had to face the terrifying prospect of explaining to the housemaster what had befallen his precious storeroom keys.

Breathing heavily in relief at having been spared this fate, he slowly resumed his way in the spring sunshine down the road towards the classroom block and the wagtail flew away. He paused beset by a curious thought. Would the keys actually have fallen in the drain in any case, even if they had landed on it? Might they have been too large? There was only one way to find out and he approached one of the drain covers.

While he lowered the keys gingerly through the drain slat it was apparent that each one would fit down and would probably have fallen in. As a bunch, though, they might have rested on the top. He was so relieved not to have taken a shot at the wagtail, risking losing the keys and having to face his terrifying housemaster.

Satisfied with his reprieve, he tugged to lift the bunch of keys from the drain. Most came out easily but the largest, with a long shaft, got caught on the bar, pulling against his grasp and causing him to let go of the bunch. He scrabbled desperately to retrieve them but they slipped from his sweaty fingers into the drain. It seemed an eternity before he heard the murky plop as they fell into the slime.

In his terror, as he walked to his fate, he could not even remember which of the drains held the precious keys.

The Chaplain

Reverend Goode, the School Chaplain, spent several weeks teaching "the facts of life" using slides of copulating chickens. The fourteen-year-old had volunteered to become confirmed and, after weeks of preparation, he thought himself ready. During the Confirmation classes, in addition to using the chickens, Rev. Goode emphasised what was involved in becoming an adult member of The Church and the privilege that would be endowed upon the candidates by being entitled to Holy Communion. The boy's parents lived two hundred miles away and would not be in attendance during this important rite of passage but he embraced it with wholehearted commitment. A member of the chapel choir and a firm believer, he had been whispering his prayers privately each night in the solitude of his bed in the senior dormitory. The secrecy was necessitated by having to share space with thirty teenaged boys of whom he was one of the youngest, the oldest being eighteen and effectively men. Teasing and even bullying were rife so, in order not to expose himself to ridicule, he largely kept his thoughts and his prayers to himself. In addition, the thing that really troubled him could not be shared; he had never told a soul. Most of these lads had developed a sceptical disdain for religion but he found great solace and hope in the thought that there was a higher power that might make things better. Sensitive and introverted, he struggled to make friends but he felt he had a friend in Jesus. Though socially and physically immature for his age, spiritually he felt ready. He was prepared to assume the mantle of adult church membership.

He knew that he had to prepare his confession list. It had not been difficult to compile as he had been brought up strictly and had learned to be well behaved and law-abiding. With the exception of the thing that tortured him most, there was nothing to tell. One thing above all else that he had taken from his parents is that he could not tell a lie. One lie led to another he had been assured and in the end the lies became bigger and bigger and you got caught out. It just wasn't worth it. There was photographic evidence in the family that he had "borrowed" someone else's tricycle when he was about three years old but even he didn't think that would concern The Almighty. There really wasn't much to get off his chest other than the one heavy burden that he had carried with him throughout much of his young life. How could he ever confess to what he had done to that little girl? But how could he live with himself if he didn't.

***

As an eight-year-old he spent his days happily playing with his brother who was a year younger. They lived in Singapore where their father had been a Royal Navy deep-sea diver. Their easygoing time was spent with other children wandering into the jungle, watching red ants fighting their white foes, building dens from palm fronds and befriending local kids from the nearby village. He developed an early taste for Asian street food and enjoyed the open-air cinema whenever it was on. It was a carefree life in the tropics where even monsoon rains merely provided a further means of play in the torrents that poured invitingly through the storm drains. During these prelapsarian days, school was endured in the morning only and the afternoons were spent at play or at the beach with their mum and little sister.

Fourteen-year-old Arthur, one of the older boys who lived on the Royal Navy married quarters estate knew more about the world than they did. Taller, stronger and much more grown up, he immediately commanded the respect of the young brothers. Arthur was quite definitely the leader and organizer of the games. It was he who showed them how to cut and tie the palm branches to build the jungle dens and the boy still has the scar from the cut on his thumb that was almost severed with a sharp sheath knife. It was Arthur who was yelling at the front of the gang of around fifteen or twenty little boys playing cowboys and Indians, running through the estate when the massive German Shepherd leapt a fence and came straight for the lad, biting his backside and sending him to the hospital for tetanus.

Arthur was in the thick of everything and the boy and his young brother were enthralled by him. There was nothing he suggested that they wouldn't do and nowhere he led that they wouldn't follow. He was going to teach them some basic lessons in the facts of life. This was entirely new terrain and they became really excited. Grown-ups told them nothing so now they were to find out.

"How would you like to make a baby?" he challenged. "I can show you what to do."

Of course they were excited so Arthur duly invited his five-year-old sister to come for a game in the tall grass. Like so many of those days full of play, this was a pleasantly warm afternoon. The grassy area was just a short walk from where they lived and was totally unseen from the houses. Arthur explained that the act of making a baby could not be accomplished while dressed so he instructed the three younger children to remove all of their clothes. This they duly did, trusting him completely and when all three were fully naked he set to work arranging their bodies in a clumsy parody of adult sex. The young brothers had no idea about what they were supposed to be doing but, having bathed with their little sister every day of their young lives, the sight of a naked little girl was not unusual to them. The little boy lay on top of the little girl. Neither said a thing but he thought about his sister. It just didn't seem right. Arthur thought it was hilarious. This inconsequential act haunted the boy, though, throughout his young life. He was unable to shake off the image of the naked body of that little five-year-old girl; a little girl, like his sister. At that moment he could not articulate it but he knew viscerally that something about it was wrong. Arthur's sister hadn't complained and she didn't seem hurt but she didn't seem to enjoy the game very much either.

Though the event had been innocent and ineffectual, this was no solace for him. With each passing year he increasingly thought of that game as a sexual assault of an innocent, unwitting child and he carried the heavy burden of guilt from that eight-year-old moment through to his teens. He had been able tell no-one and could not unburden his soul of its guilt. He and his brother never mentioned it and he carried it alone for six long years.

***

The Confirmation service was conducted by the Right Reverend Bishop of Bury St Edmunds and Ipswich. The boy was impressed with this title, which gave the ceremony a gravitas that justified his every expectation. The Right Reverend delivered a solemn, if pompous, peroration on the significance and privilege of Confirmation and to becoming a communicant and his signature appeared on the ceremoniously presented copies of The New Testament.

The time came in the service for the candidates to confess, to unburden themselves to God and to cleanse themselves by acknowledging their sins. They were all expecting this and had been advised to prepare their lists. He had been preparing for this moment and he had his short list of tricks he had played on classmates as well as when he lied about what had happened to his homework. No-one would hear these private crimes but how was he going to seek to unburden the guilt for the crime of sexual assault that he had carried for years? He knew by now that it couldn't have been rape but he still cursed himself as an abuser of an innocent child. The fact that he was a child himself when it happened had never served as mitigation for him. There was to be no public shaming, though, and all were invited to kneel and to confess in private prayer. God would hear confessions of sin silently and in secret. It wouldn't be enough though. He needed to hear forgiveness.

Before the moment of confession, the Reverend Goode coughed self-consciously before he spoke.

"I imagine, boys, that you will all have prepared as you were told and you have thought of what you wish to confess to Our Lord. It is important that you are contrite and that you truly ask forgiveness for the sins and misdemeanors you are about to confess. It should be sufficient for you to pray in silence to Our Father and you will be forgiven. There may be one or two of you who are carrying a heavier burden and who would like to have a private confessional hearing with me to relieve their guilt." He paused a moment, smiling benignly before continuing. "I am not expecting this to be the case but if there are any robbers or murderers among you, please remain behind after the service."

Robber, no. Murderer, no. What about molester of innocent children?

The boy realized from his self-satisfied smirk that this was the chaplain's little joke but such was the burden he had carried for six years of his young life and such was his unquestioning faith in the authority of the Holy Church that he thought this was his chance for atonement so he waited. The thought of sharing his secret with the chaplain worried him. How would he judge him? How despicable a creature would he find him? Would he be able to find it in him to forgive him? How could he ever look at Rev Goode again knowing that he would have seen into his darkest, dirty secret? Despite his fear of shame and condemnation, he waited.

The service ended, the chapel emptied, the chaplain escorted the bishop to the vestry and bade his farewells to the congregation and still the frightened boy waited. By now he was alone; one small fourteen year old seated in the vast imposing church. When Reverend Goode returned he had removed his cassock and had put on his sports jacket. He was not expecting to find anyone and when he saw the boy a fleeting look of dismay and irritation briefly chased the relief from his face.

"What is it boy? Why are you still here?" His tone did not make the boy any less nervous but it was too late to run. He had committed.

"Confession, Sir. You said to stay behind if we wanted to make a bigger confession."

"Yes, well? Do you wish to confess to The Lord with my help?"

"Yes sir, please sir. I have something on my mind that I just can't shake off and I feel so bad about it, Sir." He was shaking with nerves and the scowl of the chaplain was not helping.

"Very well. Follow me," he snapped, walking away.

The Chaplain led the way to the Lady Chapel behind the main altar where there was a single pew. Above and beyond, the pew was dwarfed by an elaborate gilded mosaic mural.

Featuring the nativity and a naked baby Jesus with the Virgin Mother, this imposing work stretched high into the vaulted Lady Chapel. Reverend Goode instructed the boy to kneel while he took a chair opposite. At this point the boy was invited to share his sin and to unburden his soul.

This was the moment he desired and the moment he feared. Though he had formed them in his mind so often, it seemed so difficult to find the words to tell this irascible man. He hadn't expected sympathy but he had hoped for a rather warmer listener. Eventually he managed to speak of the events of that sunny tropical day so long ago and what he remembered as the sexual molestation of Arthur's five-year-old sister. Through bitter tears, he explained how he had carried this guilt and how he knew that this must be a mortal sin. He wanted to enter God's church as a clean adult, free from all that had sullied his conscience for six long years. He had wished to confess his offence before God and that is why he had sought a private audience. He had never felt so alone and so ashamed. He had never been able to tell anyone of his guilt. He struggled to find his handkerchief to control his runny nose and to wipe his tears.

Firmly, the imperious Chaplain instructed him to remain on his knees in serious self-examination and contemplation and to wait while he prepared himself to make absolution. The boy allowed his eyes to follow the huge and overpowering gilded mosaic in front of him and above his head. The Virgin Mary, cloaked in flowing pacific blue, held the baby Jesus surrounded by a field of golden panels. Meanwhile, the cleric turned to remove some items from a small locked safe behind his chair. Over his severe black cassock he placed the pure flowing white surplice, the symbol of the righteousness bestowed by Jesus on those tending the flock as well as their followers. The boy had seen this uniform often though he had rarely seen what followed as Reverend Goode topped it off with a long stole in vibrant scarlet interlaced with golden embroidery. This long scarf, his symbol of office, hung vertically down over both sides of his shoulders and extended to the knees. The fearful formality was unnerving and the boy was terrified of what might be about to follow. Shaking, he bowed his head and shrank into himself, diminished.

The servant of God stood over the boy and, holding a large Bible firmly in his hands, he solemnly intoned the following words of the absolution prayer, "May our Lord and God, Jesus Christ, through the grace and mercies of his love for mankind, forgive you all your transgressions. And I, an unworthy priest, by his power given me, forgive and absolve you from all your sins, in the name of the Father and of the Son and of the Holy Spirit. Amen."

Thus was the young sinner forgiven, absolved and dismissed. There were no consoling words to lessen the sense of guilt and no reassuring arm across the shoulder.

The chaplain went home at last to his gin and tonic.

The Beginning

I was broken, as broken as a time-served ex convict would have been after half a life sentence and yet my adult life was just starting. After being shut away for nearly eight years in a strict boys only boarding school, I didn't understand girls or anything much. I had no idea how female humans worked or how to behave towards them. They scared me although I had a few failed flings in the years before starting at teacher training college.

I was excited and terrified in equal measures about studying in a mixed environment. And then in our first seminar you arrived. I can't say I met you then because you seemed aloof, self confident, self-assured. You didn't spare me a glance.

My first sight of you so seared my consciousness that I can't shake it. You entered the seminar room, chatting to some other girls and you seemed to own the space. That September morning was sunny and warm and there was no need for jacket or coat so your perfect figure was framed at its best. You wore a cream, flared-sleeved low-neck top with burgundy stripes. It was a tight fit and the v-neck enhanced your figure to great advantage. Your long shapely legs in black tights and calf length maroon suede boots were accentuated by the matching mini skirt. Such was the impact of your figure that it was a while before I noticed your face framed in unusual fashion by your long, thick, black hair. It was tightly bound in two thick plaits gathered in hoops by your ears. Thus framed, your face with its olive tan betrayed a summer spent in the sun and the hint of oriental about your hazel eyes suggested some exotic heritage. Intimidated, I avoided eye contact.

***

The chairs were arranged in a circle in the same room where I first saw you a few days earlier. There were ten of us, only three men, in the dull, unadorned 1960s built seminar room.

Our tutor was Dr. Ray Cowell, the Dean of Faculty. Though we were studying Modern English Literature, in his wisdom he had chosen for our study, *Fathers and Sons,* a nineteenth century Russian novel by Turgenev.

Avuncular and likeable, Ray managed to draw something from almost all of the students but didn't need to try hard with me. Three years older than the other freshers, in this context, I was overconfident and over-ready with opinion. You, though, insouciant with your air of unflappable, unsmiling self-confidence, said nothing other than whispered asides to the girl sitting next to you. You chose not to contribute.

Ray wanted us to read a few pages of the text in turn.

"Nadia," he said, "given your East European background, you might know better how to pronounce some of the names. Perhaps you could start us off?"

"No." Just that. No explanation, excuse or apology was forthcoming. "No."

Ray didn't force the issue but just moved on.

***

The following Tuesday afternoon Ray presented the first of four compulsory lectures for the sixty or so members of our year.

"This is the first of our sessions where I have asked for all members of every seminar group, to meet together. Compulsory lecture sounds rather officious for what I intend but I wanted you all to be here because I'd like to give a common foundation to each group's first term.

"I'm going to talk to you today on the subject of Shakespeare in general, his work, his importance and his themes. It would really help me if you felt you could ask the occasional question or make a point as we go along. I don't want it to be too formal so feel free to chip in. Just shout out. It would break up the monotony of my voice and also give me a chance to grab a drink of water." He looked over the gathering with a warm smile and commenced.

After twenty minutes I took him at his word and asked my first question – something about how Shakespeare's characterization of women is understood now in the light of the growing feminist movement. Ray was gracious and answered fully and respectfully, as he did for my other three evenly spaced interventions. If he found me irritating, he did not show it. No-one else asked anything. The lecture ended.

***

We had been chilling in Barry's room, listening to Hendrix and Grateful Dead and smoking dope since the end of Ray's lecture that afternoon. The boys had teased me about being "up myself", interrupting "the prof" with my "clever-clever" stuff but everyone eventually chilled until the moon appeared to lie on its belly.

Barely dusk, it seemed. I wasn't too clear headed. Last time I had looked through the window it appeared to be daytime but I had been here for hours in Barry's room. My mind had stopped thinking straight some time ago. I was confused by what I saw when I looked again. The moon was clearly shining brightly but I'd never seen it at that angle before.

I was staring and trying to process the sight of the hemispherical source of light shining brightly in the sky. It seemed like a half moon but the wrong way up. I called the guys to check it out.

"Guys. What's happening? How do you get a moon that shape?"

Simon came over and looked where I pointed. He hadn't been smoking.

"You serious?" he asked, looking straight into my eyes to gauge my expression.

Putting his arm over my shoulder, he called the others, laughing.

"Dave's just seen the street light outside the window. He thinks the moon has fallen over."

Barry and Steve both joined in laughing at me.

Steve suggested going to the bar because the Tuesday night disco would be starting but I wasn't sure I could handle it after all the weed. I was feeling hypersensitive after the stick I'd been taking, my self-consciousness strengthening to paranoia. Maybe a pint of Guiness or two would be the answer. Under Simon's guidance and protection, we walked the hundred yards to the Union bar.

***

All these noisy people -   dark shapes against the gloom - fag smoke clouds drift across the lights - choking - no space anywhere - pounding beats from the disco and voices yelling to be heard - alone in the crush   - laughter - hostile or just ignoring me -   couldn't tell - not my normal paranoia   - like alien claustrophobia

Simon has gone to the bar   -   left me here alone   -   the others are in the loo - or maybe they have just abandoned me - alone - don't know what to do with myself - no-where to sit -   just standing - swaying with the pack   - held up by others' shoulders   - reeling in the dark   -   cacophonous morass of dark silhouetted youth - crushing - the noise - should never have come

Appearing between two shapes looms a guy from my block. Yorkshire lad. He seems glad to see me and smiles as he calls out.

"Ay up, mate. Where's t'others?"

He means our other block-mates. I'm vague in my disinterested reply

"Don't know. Go away. Waiting for…"

He doesn't stick around

Then you are there. Approaching me. You aren't smiling. In my stoned state your face seems like an alluring oriental moon. Awestruck and slightly intimidated, I can only nod.

"Hi," I hear you say. " Did you know what you were talking about this morning?"

Why would you challenge me? You don't know me. I'm confused.

"What do you mean? What are you suggesting?"

"The lecture. Did you get it?"

"Yes I got it. Why, did you think I was talking out of my arse? You taking the piss?"

Such an aggressive response but so defensive.

You walk away. The first time you had spoken to me.

***

I struggled to make it for breakfast that Wednesday morning but as I joined the long queue I found myself right behind you. You were talking to Maureen, the beautiful brunette from our seminar group. You didn't turn round and you hadn't seen me arrive so this gave me a chance to compose myself before speaking to you. I was aware only vaguely of the evening before. I couldn't recall our brief conversation. What I did remember though was that I had been rude and I needed to put it right and apologise. I coughed and you turned round.
"Oh it's you! Hi" Understandably, once again, you were not smiling.
"Look, Nadia isn't it?" This was so hard. I was so shy and so embarrassed. "Nadia, I think I was rude to you at the bar last night and I wanted to apologise. I can't remember too much about it to be honest but I think I might have sworn at you. Really, I'm so sorry. That isn't me, really."
" Yeah, you were a bit of a shit actually," you returned. "I must say I was surprised. I only asked if you knew what Dr Cowell was going on about. It all seemed a bit deep but you seemed to be following him okay and I hadn't got a clue."
"Wait. Hang on. You asked if I knew what *he* was talking about?"
"Yes, what did you think I said? I don't get why you would react like that?"
As you repeated the question something clicked. "I thought you were asking if I knew what *I* was talking about and that you were suggesting I was talking bollocks. I took offence. Sorry. Really I was off my head, if I'm honest. I think dope makes me a bit paranoid. I'm really sorry for being so shitty."
"You'd been smoking weed? Okay. That explains why you were so weird, I suppose. Does that mean you've got some?"
"Dope? Yeah, well, I can get it. Why? Do you want a smoke?"

"Of course. Maybe we can get together and share a joint. Do you know how to roll up?"

"Yeah, that's no problem. Let's fix up a time later."

"Why don't you come up to my room this evening?" you countered. " I'll be there with Maureen and we can have a smoke together."

"Deal. Once again, I'm sorry about last night. Misunderstanding. See you later this evening."

***

I'm starting to sweat as I stare helplessly at the messy tetris pattern of Rizzlas I've spread across your desk. I've tripped myself up again with my boastful lie. I had never made a joint; always waited for it to be passed to me. I've watched though. I'm supposed to do something with licking and sticking a few together and then one goes across the top and you bite the edge to help it stick with spit.

You and Maureen are sitting on your bed chatting animatedly while awaiting my miracle creation.

I have to do something with a strip of cardboard for a roach, then stick a pin in the resin to heat up the corner with my lighter. I'm starting to panic.

Your conversation stops and you notice the mess I am in. Your laughter attracts Maureen and you are both beside yourselves. You each have your hands to your mouths in amusement and there seems no end in sight to your fun at my expense.

"But David, you said you knew how to do it," you spluttered.

"Yeah well!"

"What? You haven't rolled up before?"

"No but I've watched loads."

"Then why did you say you had?"

"Spur of the moment thing. I didn't want to disappoint. I suppose I was bragging a bit I guess."

Somehow I managed to fashion something that approximated to a very loose fat joint and we managed to keep it intact whilst sharing a smoke.

That was just the first time I had failed to meet your high expectations and it certainly was not going to be the last; the first stumble at the beginning of a long journey. There were to be many more as "you taught me how to bend instead of break".

Our evening with Maureen was not a very romantic first date but that was almost fifty-three years ago and five years before we were married. In that time, again in the words of B. B. King, "You took a broken man and made him whole."

Homecoming

It is close to midnight. As I stand watching from the doorway of the train, it seems as if the very gates of Hell had been opened and all of its elements disgorged. The black air chokes of sulphur, the taste of soot and the fiery melting of metal. Somewhere fires are burning, possibly braziers as a distinct blood red glow tinges the scene. Gargantuan black machines, seeming alive and belching steam, slowly, noisily shunt back and forth as if on some diabolical mission. The screeching of metal on metal pierces my eardrums and my head is crushed with the cacophony of the squealing brakes of muscular steam locomotives and the hammering of scarcely visible workers. And yet there is light. Bright arc lights illuminate the scene allowing the railway workers to see what they are doing. Their shadows are projected on the walls as giants of the revolution, portraying the essence, the imaginings of my burgeoning idealism. The searing light penetrates the grey smoke and mist and reveals what is to me a scene of heroism. The actions of the workforce are replicated in vast posters that hang on the walls of this cavernous hanger. In socialist realist style featuring much revolutionary red, they depict mighty well defined bodies of Stakhanovite workers with long handled lump hammers and spanners astride representations of Planet Earth. Each one proclaims "PEACE" in every recognisable language. Here there is light.

My first encounter with the USSR. I am seeing what I had hoped to see: the power of the proletariat and the proclamation of peace. I have arrived. After several days' journey by rail, I have finally reached the Soviet Union. From here the gauge of the tracks are different so there is time to kill while the wheels and bogies are altered. Here for an hour or so, overwhelmed with wonder, I can enjoy the play extempore of the manifestation of the power of the proletariat.

***

It had been a long journey to get this place. It would not have happened were it not for the invitation of my father in law, Ivan Euphimovich. Nadia and I had been married for just a year. I suspected for most of the five years that I had known Ivan that I would not have been his first choice for his daughter. He often spoke admiringly of 'mighty blokes' he had known and it was probable that he harboured hopes of a match with a member of the Ukrainian ex-patriot community. Of very slight build and barely beginning to fill out into manhood, I could not be described as 'mighty' by the most generous imagination. Nevertheless I had indeed married the daughter of Ivan Euphimovich.

Nadia was the most precious part of his life. He had nurtured her, helped to develop her education, endowed her with his culture and brought her to the brink of womanhood. He had taught her Russian, she accompanied him on piano whilst he sang Ukrainian folk songs in his strong bass baritone voice and she had embraced the culture of his homeland having visited his family in Terny where he was born. Her physical features were also reminiscent of his heritage. She wore her dark straight hair long down her back, she was slim and shapely and there was something in her pretty oval face, her eyes and complexion that hinted of eastern Russia and an exotic link to his ancestors. She was going to be a teacher. She was spirited and cultured. She would also one day be a mother: in his mind, the completion of womanhood. He was so proud of her and he wanted a 'mighty bloke' for her but she married me.

Ivan Eupimovich could be argumentative and difficult, not overly concerned about hurting people's feelings. Nevertheless, his life experiences had imbued in him a deep fear and suspicion of authority and he was uneasy about his daughter marrying a communist. He worried for their safety.

Nadia and I had been together for about five years and our getting married was almost a forgone conclusion. Neither of us remembered proposing; it just had not seemed necessary. I insisted, though, that I should formally seek permission from Ivan Euphimovich to marry his daughter. His response to my request surprised me.

He and I frequently sat late into the night at the dining table in his back room where he would repeat the story of his life's struggles over several glasses of Bells. With this Dutch courage, I chose one of those moments to raise the subject. I put down my whisky glass and looked directly at him.

"Ivan," I started hesitantly, "I want to ask you something. It is really important to me."

"Mmm? What you want?" Despite living for more than twenty five years in Devon, Ivan's pronunciation was still thick with a tart East European flavour that often seemed brusque.

"Well," I continued nervously, "Nadia and I love each other and have talked about our future together. I would dearly like to marry her and I think she will have me. I would like your permission to propose to her. I hoped that you would agree. What do you say?"

"What you want?" he repeated, his small eyes, staring unsmiling, challenging me.

Confused, I sought clarification, "I don't follow you, Ivan. What do you mean about 'want'?"

"What future? What you want, bloomin', for future?" *Bloomin'* was his frequent filler word in sentences in order to avoid swearing.

"We don't really have any great ambitions," I struggled on. "We don't want grand houses or material things. We just want to be happy."

"Happy? What right you got to be happy, bloomin' stuff?" he spat out with a barely concealed snarl.

This unexpected reply has stayed with me all my life.

What right to be happy? Given the state of the world, that was a very difficult question to answer and I let it hang in the air.

He knew better than to go against his daughter's wishes so we were married.

Besides Ivan's affection for his daughter, his love of his motherland, Ukraine, defined the man. He had been born in 1915, two years before the Revolution and had lived in exile for most of the past thirty years up to this time, having been taken to Germany in 1941 from his village, Terny, as forced labour. The Nazis came for his nephew, Boris Petrovich, but as the young man was soon to be married, Ivan stepped up to go in his place. Short but powerfully built with thick black hair, he was dark, strong and as handsome as a Hollywood heartthrob. Possibly as a result of the material and emotional impoverishment of his early childhood, though, he could not connect with others and he had no amorous ties that would make it difficult for him to leave Ukraine.

Until the end of the war he was forced to work as a farm labourer in harsh conditions. Rations were scant and on more than one occasion he was badly beaten for speaking out in protest. Despite this he felt happier in Germany and freer than he had been at home in his village where life had been even harder. When war ended he began to make his way home. At some point on that journey he made a momentous decision with far reaching consequences for his future. He turned his back and walked west. He didn't want to go home.

For more than sixteen years, Ivan Euphimovich lived in ignorance of his family in Ukraine and his family assumed him dead.

***

Young Alexei Trophimovich left the engine of his motorbike and sidecar ticking over as he reported for duty. His khaki KMZ machine was both his pride and joy and the tool of his trade but he had no fear of it being stolen as he stepped into the small shop that served as Terny's Regional Post Office. Everyone knew Alyosha and everyone knew his bike. The village covered a vast area around the collective farm and this machine was the oil of communication. Clean-shaved Alyosha, like most of his contemporaries, wore his hair as a crew cut. He was a handsome and powerfully built young man who commanded the respect and admiration of the entire community. It was he who delivered their letters, newspapers and important government documents. His role was more than that of the village postman. He loved his job and his life patrolling the far-flung settlements over many miles and throughout every season. He had connections and folk depended on him.

As he collected the day's deliveries from Irina Pavlova, the manager of the Post Office, he paused noticing that she had singled out a flimsy piece of blue paper. She looked puzzled as she handed it to him separately from the other bundles.
"What's this Ira? I've not seen this kind of thing." He scrutinised the unfamiliar document and its strange heading 'AIR MAIL' in printed Roman alphabet.
"It has your name on it though, Alyosha. "That is why I gave it to you separately. See: *Danilenko*. I don't know what it can be but it seems it is from The West."
This featherlight aerogramme from England did bear the name Danilenko. The address, written in Ukrainian in Cyrillic script in a spidery hand merely stated *Family Danilenko, Terny Post Office, Poltava Oblast, Ukraine SSR.*
His family name was indeed Danilenko but he was confused. Why would there be something from abroad bearing his name? Terny was an isolated community with no international standing and there had been no letters from overseas before. It was not addressed to him individually and there were many branches of the family in the locality so how could he know where to deliver it? He decided to take the letter home after work to his father, Trophim Euphimovich. As an elder in the community he would know how to respond.
As he drove the dirt tracks through the forest and the valleys the letter played on his mind. Nobody he knew had any contact with other countries. Generations of peasants here had worked on the land and, after the revolution, mainly at the collective. Since the Great Patriotic War the countryside had settled into its routine and nobody travelled any further than Poltava, the "county town". He recalled stories of his father's brother, Ivan Euphimovich, who had been taken by the Nazis during occupation over fifteen years ago but no-one had heard of him since. Everyone assumed he had been killed and his stepmother continued to claim compensation for him as a casualty of war.
Alyosha lived with his brother Vitka and his parents in a single storey two-roomed thatched adobe dwelling. As he arrived home, he could smell the garlic, dill and onions of the borscht being cooked at the petch by his mother, Polya. After he had embraced her in greeting, he sat with his father and

presented to him the mysterious letter. Trophim had been repairing his heavy coat and he put down his needle and reached out for the paper, a frown clouding his eyes.

"What is this?" he enquired as he gingerly handled the flimsy letter. "It says *Danilenko, Terny*. Strange. Some kind of mystery."

He slowly unsealed the edges to reveal its story.

Though approaching retirement age, Trophim, had been a strong man like both of his sons but the war had taken its toll on him leaving him physically and emotionally fragile. He was not prepared for what he had in his hands. His eyes welled as, once again, he heard the voice of his lost younger brother. He tried to wipe his eyes but as he read on, he submitted and the tears flowed.

Who is there? I ask. Who will know me, Ivan Euphimovich Danilenko? Is it possible that someone can contact my brothers, Ivan Euphimovich and Trophim Euphimovich? Are they still living? Can they forgive me for ...

In his short letter Ivan had explained that only now, after Kruschev's denunciation of Stalin, did he feel safe at last to contact home and that he hoped to re-establish contact. He longed to come home.

***

He first returned to his homeland more than twenty years after he had been taken. When she was old enough Nadia went too and after we were married, I also was to be introduced to his land, his people and his culture. Moreover, as a young and credulous communist, I was thrilled to have this unique opportunity to visit the USSR, the first socialist state and to the homes of its people.

We faced days of travel by rail across the continent and I felt that it was important to be able to learn a few words of the language. I knew that Ukrainians at that time generally spoke Russian as well their own language as they were neighbours and even inter-married and the languages were very similar. I felt that Ukrainian would be of little use to me anywhere else but that Russian was likely to become increasingly important on the world stage so I determined to learn. As a start, I decided to ask Ivan to teach me some words during our journey. It might help our bonding, I thought. I also hoped that, given the length of the journey, I might arrive well armed with useful phrases. He really wasn't keen to help me though except to impart one expression that he seemed to think essential. It sounded like, "Ne ponnymyoo."

Ivan was determined that I learn this phrase and he kept repeating it. "I don't understand." He was reluctant to go further and I guessed that he thought I might be in some way diminished if I was incapable of expressing myself. Nadia helped me to learn some simple phrases.

As far as Warsaw, accommodation was rudimentary but after two days we transferred to a sleeping compartment. We three travelled across Eastern Europe in a sleeping compartment of four. We didn't know the fourth person but it didn't matter. Sausage and vodka were shared and stories told. Morning tea delivered in glass cups was memorable as was a special meal of cutlets taken in the dining car. Our voyage to the east soon began to pall though. The scenery of endless forests eventually became monotonous and as the journey progressed the stench of the onboard toilets became unbearable as the water tank ran dry. And so we headed to the USSR.

By the time we reached the border we were spent. Three days of travelling with scant provision for personal hygiene was uncomfortable; perpetual motion was disorientating; endless stale air was suffocating. Small wonder then that by the time the train stopped at the border for the wheels to be changed, Ivan Euphimovich was exhausted and grumpier than usual. Nadia appeared ill. I was also tired and wondering how much more of this travelling we could take. Being disturbed in the middle of the night, missing sleep and having to delay the journey for ages was tough. I was worried about Nadia though as she was looking extremely pale and she complained of a headache and nausea. I suggested that despite the offensive stench of the toilet, we should take a walk to the end of the carriage where we might open the door windows and get some air. It was not permitted to alight from the train while the work was being done in the shunting yard but we were able to slide a window down.

***

Nadia feels that the very gates of Hell have opened. The heat, the noise, the manifold offensive smells and the acrid tastes are the very worst sensations and she is introduced to migraines for the first time in her life. Her father, tired and confused, stands beside her helpless whilst she is repeatedly sick through the window. Looking the other way, reinvigorated by the new world, I am enjoying my first encounter with the Soviet Union.

Comrade Secretary

It seemed heroic and kind of romantic to be having a wash and shave in a small pool in the forest in the early hours of a Soviet Ukrainian summer. Though there was an early chill and the nearby birch trees were agitated by the breeze, it was sufficiently mild to be able to strip to the waist and have a decent wash. As I was attempting to lather my face in the cold water a moment from Rider Haggard's *King Solomon's Mines* came to me from my childhood reading: the colonial English officers who felt it essential to show an example by keeping up appearances by shaving with a cut-throat razor in cold river water in the most challenging of privations. One had to maintain standards. Though by no means a colonial officer, I felt in some ways like an emissary in a foreign country and the political discussions that had taken place through an interpreter the previous evening, accompanied by more than sufficient Stolichnaya vodka had taken its toll on me and left me fragile. I willingly plunged my head under the refreshing water of the still pond.

***

No English visitors had ever been to Chemodanivka, (little suitcase), other than the daughter of Ivan Euphimovich. Indeed, few foreigners of any description would have had reason to be in so remote a part of rural Ukraine. In our mid twenties, Nadia and I had been married just over a year and we were making a visit – my first – to the tiny homeland village and collective farm close to where her father had been raised.

But this excursion would be made without her dad. It was Nadia and I who were the objects of the Party's interest. We were invited to the local headquarters where we were informed that we would be collected from the village for a weekend away.

Neighbours and family members were not unduly worried or alarmed when the chauffeur parked the shiny black Zil limousine incongruously on the dirt lane beside the corrugated zinc fence that surrounded the family's small brick single storey home. Chickens and ducks were scattered noisily from the dusty track. Nadia's cousin Alexei Trophimovich (Alyosha), the local postman, showed a clear disdain at the arrival of these self-important town people. Though their lives were in every way affected by the policies and deeds of the Soviet Communist Party these ordinary villagers were quite ambivalent and not wholly impressed with their visitors from the Party office. Nevertheless, this was an unusual event and one that would be spoken of for years to come by Alyosha, his wife, Katya and their neighbours.

The local Party Secretary, Comrade Leonid Nicholaivich, was charged with finding out about us. Around forty years old and dressed in a charcoal grey office suit, he had the gravitas that came with his important position. He had the wiry frame of an athlete and his eyes, whilst smiling hospitably, betrayed a knowing scepticism. He spoke no English so he had recruited Maria Yussupovna, a young teacher and member of the Komsomol as his interpreter. Also in her twenties, dark haired and dressed smartly in her striking red trousers, Maria was as duskily beautiful as she was fluent in English. Though constantly nervous and deferential to the comrade secretary, she felt privileged to be granted the honour of what she was told was an important political task. This was to become clear through the attention she gave her work and the warmth shown to Nadia and me.

As we were being ushered towards the imposing black limousine, Nadia caught an exchange between Alyosha and her father, which betrayed some possible concern. Though it was spoken in Ukrainian, her understanding of Russian enabled her to catch the meaning.

"What was that about, Nadia? Are they worried?" I whispered as we approached the car.

"Not worried, exactly but the usual suspicion of authority."

"Why, what did he say exactly?"

"Alyosha says we need to be careful. 'They will rip your tongue out,' was what he actually said. "

"Why?" I asked, "They think I'll talk too much? There's nothing I can say that they need to worry about."

"No, it's not them," Nadia explained. "They are all suspicious of all officialdom. Always have been."

I was not surprised that the local Party would take an interest us. The Soviet state had many enemies abroad and was ever vigilant.

The family accepted our departure with a shrug as we were driven away with the minimum of fuss or luggage. Ivan Euphimovich might even have been a little proud of his daughter's recognition by the Party. Though no communist, he had become ardently pro-Soviet and proud of his homeland during the thirty years he had lived in England. Not only had he endured endless personal racist abuse as a refugee by those who spoke largely out of ignorance but he had also had to endure the cold war hostility towards his motherland.

At first we had no idea where we were being taken but after a while Leonid Nicholaivich explained that we were heading to the forest of Putyvl , approximately forty miles to the north as the crow flies. It was here that Ukrainian men and women had fought a fearless rearguard action behind enemy lines during Nazi occupation during "The Great Patriotic War". These partisans lived, fought and died in the forest in hostile conditions and still, nearly forty years after their exploits, Putyvl Forest was a sacred place, revered by Soviet people. This was where we were to have our conversation. Firstly, however, more pressing needs had to be attended to.

A diversion of forty miles to the east took us to Sumy, the "county town" of Sumskaya Oblast (region). With its fountains and classical architecture including a magnificent Orthodox church, it was deemed worthy of a tourist visit. The diversion also provided an opportunity for a memorable lunch of cutlets and other local dishes as well as the chance for shopping. Fortunately Alyosha had generously provided us with a block of currency the size of a small brick so there was no anxiety about having money to spend. The only item that I picked up though was a small silver alloy bust of Lenin, classically stern faced, which stood about the height of a milk jug. Though he had no English, Leonid Nicholaivich was able, through Maria's translation, to put us at our ease, recommend delicious food and show us the sights. He was probably amused at my choice of Vladimir Ilyich Ulyanov though the bust was to take pride of place at our table that evening. While we were picking up some souvenirs, he was making purchases of food. Although we enjoyed an excellent lunch he was aware of the need for a meal for later as we had talking to do. He bought various items of cold buffet as well as several bottles of Stolychnaya vodka and Soviet wine including the ever-popular Sovietski Champagne.

The Zil passed through endless plains of collective farmland. Long icy winters and limited resources available for road maintenance had left the stony concrete road badly pitted and in some places dangerously holed. We were both shocked, however, when our driver suddenly veered to the right, off the road, and sped along the edge of the fields kicking up a huge cloud of red dust. Avoiding the road was, we were assured, the quicker and safer way to travel.

It was a sweltering late summer afternoon and countless women were working in the fields. I was reminded of Millet's painting *The Gleaners* owing to the similarities of these Ukrainian farm-workers' postures and clothing and that of the French peasants, despite the different contexts. It was on this second leg of the journey that Leonid Nicholaivich additionally showed his resourcefulness. Twice he instructed the driver to stop and he walked across the fields, spoke with the farm-workers and returned with arms full of fresh tomatoes and cucumbers to add to the supper that evening. To the women in the fields, dressed in their traditional full skirts, aprons and coarse headscarves he must have presented an odd figure stepping over the furrows, dressed in his smart office clothes and black polished shoes.

Leonid Nicholaivich was a knowledgeable guide; on arrival he proudly told us of the partisan war behind enemy lines in the forest. There was a small museum and next to it a rudimentary hut with several basic bedrooms, a small classroom and a kitchen but no bathroom. This was a provision for study visits and would be our quarters. A short way off, across the clearing beyond the pond, stood a simple forester's cottage. As there was no village I took that to be the home of the caretaker or custodian of the museum.

Before settling for the evening we were driven around the forest and we witnessed the signs of devastation that remained even after so long, including remains of destroyed Nazi tanks. Tied to many trees were the red neck-scarves of Young Communist visitors who had left them as gestures of respect and appreciation of the sacrifices that had been made here in the war against fascism.

On our return to the hut, our host formally placed Lenin at the head of the table. It had been a long, exhausting and rewarding day so not much vodka was required to 'rip out' my tongue, particularly as I was not used to the large measures of spirit. We discussed various attitudes held in the British Party at the time and some broader issues but in the wider context of his work and Soviet international relations I would imagine it was of little significance to Leonid Nicholaivich or his Party. Nevertheless, a comradely and convivial evening was spent before we went to bed.

In the early dawn light we were aroused by birdsong and the sussuration of the birch trees. The breeze was freshening and there was a chill in the air but we went outside to wash in the small lake. With no noise save the birds and the wind in the trees it was not difficult to enjoy the tranquil atmosphere of this forest. Breathing deeply the forest air and savouring the intense calm, I lost myself in reflection of what had happened so many years ago. Where we stood, so many brave partisans had fought to the death for their country. These trees shushing in the breeze would have been smashed by the noise of tanks and horses crashing through the vegetation, the air rent by human calls and screams.

***

I was wrenched from my reverie without warning, my body shaking with the reverberation of hooves and the clatter of rough wheels. It felt and sounded like a cavalry charge. From my left, unseen, I heard the deafening roar of pounding hooves and wheels whilst from the direction of the caretaker's cottage to my right came an ear piercing shriek as a peasant woman emerged, howling desperately and running in terror towards the lane opening from where the thunderous crescendo of wheels and hooves was approaching. It was from that gap in the trees that a frantic horse emerged in a lather of sweat, hurtling headlong and pulling a flat top cart that was bouncing uncontrollably behind it. Though worried that the woman was directly in its way and in imminent danger, I was stuck rigid, helpless.

    I was dimly aware of movement over my shoulder as Leonid Nicholaivich threw down his towel and sprinted to where the horse and cart seemed bound to collide with the woman. Her howl increased as she saw that there was no driver on the cart. The Party secretary was sprinting to try to intercept the horse as it stopped suddenly, possibly recognizing its whereabouts. The force of this deceleration caused the trailer to overturn alongside the animal creating a hail of gravel shrapnel and a choking cloud of dust. The horse staggered clumsily, turned backwards and almost twisted its harnessed head in its halter.

    Still I was paralysed. Not so Leonid Nicholaivich who leapt towards the horse, took its head firmly in his strong hands and spoke to it soothingly whilst freeing the traces from the harness to release the tackle and prevent the possibility of it breaking its neck. The dust settled, the horse calmed but the woman continued to wail and stumble towards the forest track as fast as she was able, keening achingly, agonizingly, desperately past the steaming lathering horse. Moments later from the opening in the trees staggered an elderly man hobbling, panting and holding his side though seeming largely unhurt. He had been thrown from the cart when the horse had taken fright and bolted.

    As the dust settled and the summer morning regained its calm, the Party secretary, the forester and his thankful daughter embraced in gratitude, relief and celebration. Still rooted near the pond, we onlookers realized that we had witnessed a spontaneous act of selfless courage that none of us would ever forget.

Fathers and Daughters

Christmas Day 1978 and night is closing in outside the small semi-detached house where the living room curtains will soon have to be closed. It is threatening to snow outside but the coal fire glows in the hearth very close to where the three-month baby girl lies on her mat. Her arms and legs are freely kicking in the air while she happily gurgles, looking up towards her father who, mesmerized, gazes down at her. A very new dad, he is a little confused and not at all sure of what is expected of him in this situation. He places his whisky glass down by his chair, crouches closer over his daughter and begins, in a very babyish voice, to introduce himself and to speak meaninglessly to her; a simple, primitive way to start a relationship, perhaps.

He knows that soon he will be on his way home with his wife and first child. He has had a few drinks with his Christmas dinner but, not having a car he doesn't have to drive and is dependent upon a friend who has offered to collect them in the evening on Christmas Day to drive them all home.

Across the room, the baby's mother is feeling physically finished and emotionally exhausted. She has helped to cook a considerable roast beef lunch at her parents' house, the room is hot, her father seems overbearing and she needs desperately to hold her first baby. Nevertheless, she sits wearily at this battered old dark wood upright piano. It has been with the family since she learned to play as a little girl and it has survived two serious floods before its move to the current house. Dutifully, she accompanies her slightly drunk father who holds his whisky in his hand as he sings Ukrainian folk songs in his slightly slurred bass baritone voice. A post war refugee, he expected little in his life and fathered a child quite late. Now he has his grandchild at last and his beloved daughter is playing for him as he sings the songs of his homeland. He is in as good a place as he ever thought possible.

Her mother, a matronly woman in her late sixties, sits crocheting her blanket square. She is smiling contentedly. This is how it should be, everyone full up after a wonderful Christmas dinner, aglow with wine and warmed by the hearth, her first granddaughter at her father's feet and her own daughter playing for her dad. She is radiant with contentment.

The young father is also feeling the effects of the alcohol. He considers that the tremulous piano is slightly overpowering for such a small room and he is not at all sure about his father in law's drink affected vocal prowess. Nevertheless, he notes that Granny is smiling contentedly and that all seems harmonious. He is a little uncomfortable about his role here, however, so he leans in closer to his own little girl while the father and daughter continue to fill the room with emotionally rendered Ukrainian folk songs. He tries to catch the baby's smiling eyes.

"Hello you," he mutters quietly. "Hello, little Lara. I'm your daddy. You're having a nice time aren't you? Can you feel my fingers?" stretching his hand gently towards hers. "Are you smiling at me? Coo coo. You're a beautiful little girl you are......."

"Stop that! Stop it! Don't do that! Leave it alone!" yells the previously mellifluous if unsteady baritone.

The room is now silent. The pianist has turned on her stool to see what is afoot. Her mother, shocked by the shouting, has dropped her crochet and the young man crouching over the baby looks up, astounded, towards his crimson-faced father-in-law who is now glowering in his direction and pointing at the tiny infant.

"Leave it!" he cries again.

"I beg your pardon?" enquires the young father tentatively. "What do you mean?"

"Leave that child! Don't fuss with that. Don't spoil it!" The thick Ukrainian accent is accentuated by his rage and his imperfect English seems to be the reason why he depersonalizes the baby.

"I'm sorry but this is my daughter and if I want to talk to her or play with her then that is what I'll do and no-one will stop me."

The young man is normally acquiescent as he has learned to pick his battles and in the six years he has known him this is the first altercation he has had with the stubborn and opinionated patriarch. His nerves are on edge and he is shaking slightly as he faces his father in law down. He feels in some visceral way that this is a moment when he must stand his ground.

The older man takes a step towards his son in law, glowers in his face and angrily repeats himself, "You don't spoil it, you hear me. Don't muck about with that."

"I told you that this is my daughter and if I think it is right to play with her and to talk to her then that is what I will do." He can now feel his temper rising also as he makes a point of meeting the other's furious, glaring eyes.

"In my country we don't do that. We wrap it up and leave it. We don't muck about and spoil that!"

By now, the young father has gathered his tiny daughter in her shawl and is protectively holding her to his chest. Beside herself, the infant's mother is trembling with distress.

The grandmother remonstrates with her husband.

"Leave it alone!" she cries, "Let well alone; it's not for you to say. Look at what you're doing!"

He is surprised by his wife's intervention. He feels now that opinion is against him but he stands his ground.

"Put it down! Put down that and get out!" He yells at his son in law and points to the door.

By now the child's mother is between her father and her husband. He fleetingly considers asking her to choose sides but realizes instinctively that it would be the wrong thing to do and would be totally unfair.

"Get out of my house!"

"You want me to go outside and stand in the snow? Really. Are you serious?"

From past frequent emotional turmoil in his own family, including being thrown out by his father, he has developed a sangfroid response to situations like this and this does not desert him now. He seems to have gone cold as he hands his daughter to her distraught mother. She is weeping uncontrollably and the grandmother is beside herself, shocked at what is unfolding before her. He moves toward the door staring fixedly over his shoulder at his wife's smouldering father.

The older man seems to have lost control but stubbornly, there being no turning back, he bellows once more, "Go! Get out of my house you...." He somehow refrains from saying "don't come back."

As he closes the door behind him and steps out into the steady snowfall, he hopes that he doesn't have to wait long before his friend arrives to take them home. He huddles by the front door to have some protection from the icy breeze but still feels the snow as it settles on his head and shoulders. He hunches his head into his chest, plunges his hands into his pockets, stares toward the deserted residential street and waits, watching the orange glow of the street lamp illuminate the thick, gently falling snowflakes. By now the curtains are drawn closed.

***

On the way home, the baby's mother is inconsolable. She cannot stop crying. Her husband can do nothing or say nothing to comfort her. He feels calm though and almost cold as he considers what has occurred. Though he can empathise with her he cannot for some reason share his wife's torment. He is bemused, affronted and still somewhat angry at the treatment he has received but he remains calm.

"Don't worry love, it'll be all right. He will calm down and eventually apologize. Your mum will sort him out." As he says it he is not sure he believes it himself.

As she holds her baby tightly to herself, nothing can stop her from crying about the awful altercation though her husband continually, unemotionally tries to reassure her that no long-term damage has been done and that peace would be restored. The driver remains silent while he delivers them half an hour later to their front door.

The oblivious child is now asleep in her still sobbing mother's arms as they enter the house. The young husband once again promises that all will be fine and that her father would apologize. He puts the kettle on.

Around a quarter of an hour passes and they are quiet now. It seems that everything that could have been said has been said and that there is no point in discussing it and agonizing further. The quiet is broken by the shrill ringing of the telephone.

He walks across the room and picks up, "Hello?"

"You know what," a familiar Ukrainian accent intones dolefully before a slight embarrassed pause. "In my country we fight and then we laugh." She faintly hears her father's voice and nervous laugh.

There is another brief moment before the reply comes, "Apology accepted,"

He then replaces the phone in its cradle.

The English Girl

Our family's journey to Chemodanivka in Ukraine began in Exeter, England in a hire car and included air travel, Soviet Railways and a battered Moskvich estate car that brought us close to the village, the land of the ancestors. At the destination heavy summer downpours had rendered the unpaved lane too muddy to drive on so alternative plans had been made for the final leg of the journey. We arrived, tired but excited, in the tiny bucolic village and our little girls were thrilled to be on the back of an open, horse-drawn flat bed wagon.

We all became acutely aware of the air; so different to what we were used to. Surrounded by the vast fields of maize and sunflowers of the collective farm, the tiny hamlet was no-where near any source of pollution. Breathing was easy and, though earthy and plant-scented, each fragrant breath was energizing.

It was a romantic and exotic journey back in time; from a technological age to a bygone age; from a place of communication technology to a land of no communication and ancient technology. By the next morning we were to discover just how big a gulf that was.

***

"Mummy. Mummy!" Not so much as a cry or a wail; more a hoarse, desperate whimper. "Mummy, I can't breathe!"

With a mother's instinct, Nadia had heard it first. The anguished plea woke her immediately in the pitch black, stifling room. The gasping, rasping struggle for breath was coming from the large double bed across from the sofa bed where we had been sleeping. It was hot high summer in Ukraine but the windows were closed against the terror of mosquitoes. She felt me sweating beside her in the hot sultry room snoring profusely as my breathing faltered in the stuffiness. She had struggled to sleep. The feather mattress was lumpy and the air was fetid.

Our daughter couldn't breathe. The two girls were together in the huge soft bed but only six-year-old Lara, the older one, seemed to be struggling. Nadia leapt out of bed to go to her. Terrified, Lara sat on the bed panting, wheezing, sobbing in panic, chest heaving for air. She was crying uncontrollably but she could not get enough air. It was our first night in the village with the kids and already Nadia's worst fears were being realized. She knew it was foolish to bring her girls to this place; in her gut she knew it. She shouldn't have listened to her father. She shouldn't have heeded her own yearning. Yet here we were.

Though close to dawn it was still near black outside. Not pausing to worry about mosquitoes, she clasped Lara to her breast and rushed out to find some air. Rubbing my eyes and stumbling in the pitch black, I followed close behind and together we tried, by massage and cajoling to encourage our daughter to remain calm enough to breathe as we both realized that hysteria was not going to help. Lara was not the only one stressed; we both feared the worst. We seemed abandoned in the middle of nowhere with no phone, no transport and no way to get help. We felt powerless.

It wasn't long before the rest of the household was disturbed by the commotion and they heated water, sought poultices and someone sent for the local district nurse who was the only person with any medical knowledge for miles. Meanwhile the scene had become mysteriously crowded by the neighbouring babushkas who seemed to take over. One of them held onto Lara's feet and massaged them, believing instinctively, like her ancestors, that there was merit in this ancient therapy. Neither of us could believe what we were seeing. Our daughter was struggling desperately for breath, we were in fear for her life and these old women were stroking her feet. In the background, confused, helpless and afraid, their grandfather, seventy-year-old Ivan Euphimovich put a protective arm around Nina, Lara's four-year-old sister. Nadia noticed but she was speechless with fear and rage. Her clenched jaw and fixed features spoke eloquently of her anger. She had been so anxious to please him by agreeing to bring them to this place. Worse, she was angry with herself for putting her daughters in danger. Lara continued to gasp for air. Distraught, we feared we might lose her. What were we thinking bringing these little girls across a continent to such a primitive and remote environment? Nadia was trying to stay focused but her taut expression betrayed a silent fury. In pleasing her father, she had endangered her child. She was inconsolable.

***

Maria Yusupovna had been working at Nedrigailiv's secondary institute for almost ten years and was considered among the very best of their teachers. In her early thirties, she was dark haired and beautiful in her two-piece maroon polyester suit. She carried herself with the air of one who was aware of her own beauty and how highly she was regarded within her community. She was on her way home from school and intended to visit the local store for a little shopping. There was more to be had in the shops of late and it gave her great pleasure to peruse the ever-increasing choice of produce. The store, adjacent to the ubiquitous statue of Lenin, as ever, pointing to the West, was close to the modern two-storey Sula Hotel. This overlooked the small paved town square and her own flat where she lived with her husband, Valya.

As she entered the shop Maria met her old school friend, Tatyana Michaelevna. After the usual polite greetings, Tatyana asked her if she had heard the gossip about the English girl. As a teacher of English, Maria craved the opportunity to converse with native English speakers. This was a small town in a remote part of Soviet Ukraine on the route to no-where and had little to offer visitors even if they had been able to obtain a visa. Nedrighailiv rarely saw foreigners. Immediately, she was curious and she peered searchingly at her friend.

"English girl? Which English girl? There are no English here."

"Not here but Chemodanivka," Tatyana explained. "She is there with her family from England."

Chemodanivka was a tiny hamlet of around three hundred souls fifteen kilometres away but it had only a collective farm and it was even less likely to have visitors from abroad. Then it came back to her. It must have been around eight years earlier when a young couple, Nadia and David, had been visiting from England and she had met them. They were around the same age as her. The young woman's father was from this region originally and they had come to visit. The husband had been a Party member in the UK and she had been chosen by the local Party committee to accompany them on a visit to Putyvl Forest to translate for Leonid Nicholaevich, the Comrade Secretary, during their discussions. She had got on really well with Nadia and they had promised to stay in touch but throughout her whole life she had been a poor correspondent. She felt an acute pang of guilt and regret when she remembered how her failure to reply to the steady stream of Nadia's letters had caused them to cease. It must be them visiting again she realized. Who else could it be?

"I must go to them," Maria declared, agitated and suddenly seeming to be in a hurry. "How long have they been in Chemodanivka? And what about the English girl? What are people saying? What has happened? What is this gossip you mentioned? I must arrange to visit Chemodanivka immediately. Valya can drive me."

"She is not in Chemodanivka, Maria. She is with her mother at the hospital. She was taken ill a few days ago and now they are here at the hospital. Her mother is with her and her little sister is still in the village with her father and her grandfather, Ivan Euphimovich."

Maria recognized the name of Nadia's father and knew then that these were the people she had met before. Nadia's letters had mentioned both of the births of her daughters. Why had she not replied? She must go at once to the hospital.

***

Nedrighailiv District Maternity Hospital was grim. With no hot water available, it was near impossible to maintain a healthy sanitary regime. There were no doors on the long drop toilets that, though cleaned regularly, still stank. The building was surrounded by birch trees and bushes that attracted clouds of mosquitoes. Nadia was susceptible to mosquitoes, particularly in the Ukraine countryside but here there was neither escape nor any soothing balm. Swollen itching lumps covered her wrists and ankles. Despite this and the plain hospital food, she was relieved to be here with Lara. She continued, though, to feel abandoned and exasperated at not being able to contact anyone. She also felt impotent, helpless and angry.

No one escaped some part of the blame. Her father was the object of much of this anger for suggesting they visit his homeland. I was blamed too as I was never going to oppose a trip to the Soviet Union, she thought, but surely I should also have realized the dangers. Mostly, though, she was livid with herself for allowing it to happen, largely from her own yearning to return to her spiritual home, and as a result, endangering her precious girls.

There was just no way to communicate. There were no phones and no one spoke English. Fortunately her father had taught her Russian so she was able to understand the medical staff. I had hardly any Russian and no Ukrainian and I was stuck on my own nearly ten miles away with Nina and her strangely uncommunicative grandfather. We had no means by which we could speak or make plans. It was useless.

Though she had to sleep on a rickety iron bed, she had been permitted to stay with Lara and this made the situation bearable for her. The very thought of having caused her daughter to be in this primitive hell caused her agony. She spent every minute possible cuddling her and sitting outside on a simple wooden bench with her to get some air or walking with her around the grounds. Local mothers-to-be in the maternity hospital were strangely impressed and said that she was an exemplary parent to spend so much time with her child.

Despite the spartan conditions, the care that Lara received was attentive if at times unconventional. Nadia had been shocked to see the old women attempting reflexology in the village. This had not prepared her though for what she saw on entering a European hospital in the twentieth century. She was astonished to see the medical staff practising the ancient art of cupping. They lit tapers inside glass cups and placed them on Lara's back. Nadia was aghast to see the hideous disfiguring of ugly purple, red and near black circular weals that they left on her little girl. 'What kind of quackery is this?' she thought. 'What kind of backwater have we come to?'

More orthodox treatment followed, though, including a fairly modern nebulizer. Lara began to breathe more easily and she was clearly getting better. A full recovery was only a matter of a week or so. She was diagnosed as being allergic to feathers and dust mites and she also had asthma.

"A twentieth century disease," the head doctor had called it.

In our relief, we began to consider our next steps after she would be discharged from hospital. We realized clearly that the cause of the illness lay in the family home.

The hospital authorities prohibited Lara from returning to stay in the village. There were only two rooms in the tiny self-built brick cottage where the family had been staying in Chemodanivka and six people had been sleeping there. The pillows, the eiderdowns and even the thick lumpy mattress were all stuffed with untreated feathers. The windows were closed against mosquitoes and the August temperature was unforgiving so the air was stale. Lara had had no chance of being able to sleep there. As there was no-where else, she was to continue to stay in this grim hospital until the scheduled flight back to England, booked for around fifteen days later. There was no other option. Nadia was allowed to stay. Little Nina and I would have to continue with her grandfather to stay at the house of Alexei Trophimovich (Alyosha), his nephew. We would not be able to communicate as there were no phones. I promised to visit every day with Nina on the local bus.

Her loyalty to her father was severely tested as she feared for our child. Ironically, her father, a refugee of war, had seemed more confident back in England, his adopted but alien country than here. A native of this place but, overwhelmed by the situation, he seemed clueless. She sensed from something he had said to her that their relatives felt that they were making rather a fuss. They seemed to view Lara's illness as a weakness, some failing in the English. Was her father's loyalty to her being compromised in some way? Nadia had had enough. She couldn't face another two weeks of this. She just had to get us home. There had to be a way. She implored me to arrange an earlier flight to get us out of this nightmare.

Though it was 1985, the only way to call any individual or business either within or outside the country was to go to the official exchange and arrange an appointment to use a telephone kiosk and have the telephonist connect the call. With Ivan Euphimovich as my interpreter, I tried hard to arrange an earlier flight. There were many more people wishing to make calls than there were lines available so the queues were lengthy. Despite innumerable attempts, it proved impossible to contact Aeroflot, the state airline. Yet another communication breakdown. I was eventually informed by an officious telegraph operator that the 12th World Festival of Youth and Students was currently taking place in Moscow and no flights would be available. We were stuck until the scheduled date. Panic intensified. Nadia was disconsolate, consumed with impotent rage.

***

The second she saw her, Nadia recognised Maria in her maroon suit striding purposefully towards her along the hospital corridor. Her sense of relief was overwhelming. Maria: a capable, English speaking friendly face. A guardian angel.

"Nadia, Nadia, how can it be? I did not know!" She dropped her school bag, kissed Nadia repeatedly all over her face and wrapped her arms so tightly that it seemed she would never let go.

"Oh Maria, how wonderful. How did you know we were here? It is so amazing to see you and you just haven't changed: as beautiful as ever. I just can't begin to tell you what a joy it is to see you." She broke down, her body racked with uncontrollable sobbing as her face, initially beaming with smiling relief, seemed to melt in tears.

"Tell me, Nadia, what has happened? Where is your little girl? Are you being cared for? Is she getting better? How long will it be? Where is the rest of your family?"

They went through to Lara and Nadia explained what had happened in Chemodanivka.

"What can I say, Maria? You know Chemodanivka. You have been to my cousin's house; you have seen how basic it all is. My dad wanted us to bring the kids and I thought it would be OK. What was I thinking? Though it has been so long since my last visit, you know I can't stay away. But the kids are so young. And then Lara couldn't breathe and I thought she was going to die," she broke off, trembling.

Maria stepped purposefully in front of her, "But what happened, Nadia? How did Lara get ill? Who was able to help you?"

"I don't know how but someone managed to get to the kholhoz to get a jeep. It was so awful; she was struggling so much. I had to leave Nina behind with David and my dad. He doesn't speak the language. I don't know what will happen." Again she broke off, unable to speak through her crying.

"What are the doctors saying, Nadia? How long will Lara be here? Will you return to Chemodanivka to rejoin your family?"

"We can't," she continued, wiping her eyes on her sleeve. "The house is not fit for Lara because of the air and the feathers. David and Nina are stuck there. They come on the bus each day but we can't get hold of anyone and we can't get an earlier flight home so we are stuck like this. It is a nightmare."

"What about Ivan Euphimovich, Nadia? What about your father? Has he not family here? Are there no other relatives who can help?"

Nadia's sigh betrayed a depth of despair that surprised even her. "Oh Maria, he can't help. He has always seemed so strong. I have always depended on him and trusted his instincts but he just seems so weak now; so confused. He is as scared as we are. I need his strength so much and it is not there. Oh I feel so irresponsible and careless to be in this position. I have no idea what to do."

Maria held Nadia's shuddering shoulders, not knowing how to respond to her desperation.

"I hate it Maria. I just hate it here. Nothing works properly. I need to get these children home. Why did I ever think of bringing them?" She sank to a chair with her head in her hands, defeated.

"Oh Nadia, how can I help? I would like you to stay in my flat but it is not possible. The floors have been painted and it is really awful with chemical fumes and even we cannot sleep there. To my mind it would not be good for Lara. It would make her sick again. What can we do?" She and her husband, she explained, were staying along the road at her mother's cottage until the chemical smell went.

"But there is the hotel," she continued. Maria had clearly worked out a possible solution. "Perhaps you will be allowed to stay there until you can come to me."

Hotel Sula, named after the river that ran through the town, was right across the street from her ground floor apartment. In several days the toxicity of the floor paint should have sufficiently dispersed. In the meantime, she could feed them in order not to have to pay restaurant prices. So it was decided. The doctors agreed to the arrangement and the rest of the family moved into the hotel. Uninvited, Nadia's father stayed in his own village in the house built by his nephew.

***

Standing behind her imposing desk beneath the prominent bas-relief portrait of Vladimir Ilyich Lenin, Olga Sergeyevna, the hotel manager, coldly efficient and brusque in her dark navy blue uniform, was nevertheless accommodating as she welcomed our family. As it was a very new hotel there had been few visitors thus far and certainly no foreigners. The interior was painted predominantly with whitewash and there was a pungent smell of slightly damp new plaster. The room we were allocated was clean and modern with a window onto the street from where we could see Maria's apartment opposite. We had relief from mosquitoes by using the spiral smoky repellents brought from home. It was a large room with two double beds, a sitting area and a dining table. Most importantly, there was also a conventional toilet. Glass fronted dressers in the best ebony coloured varnish, Soviet style, held an interesting range of delicate and ornate crockery, glasses and other items; far more than we could ever need or want to use. Indeed, during our four-day stay we used little because we did not prepare food in the room. Maria, true to her word, provided food and occasionally we bought snacks from the bakery next door.

After four or five days, Lara was medically discharged from the care of the hospital, Maria's flat was ready and we moved across the road. It was a small apartment with two rooms, a kitchen and a bathroom with a toilet. It would not have been possible for everyone to sleep there. Valya went to stay with his father in one direction and Maria went to her mother's in the other. Before they left each evening, though, Maria presented a feast of exquisite Ukrainian dishes including pelmeni, cutlets, buckwheat and borscht. Every meal was followed by a selection of delicious homemade pastries and desserts. Valya's *khorilki* was second to none and during the week or so that remained, I developed a strong taste for this fiery homemade vodka.

Nadia finally found some peace. In Maria's flat she was able to find some sense of normalcy. Having exclusive use of Maria's bedroom, the girls could play together and Nadia was able spend time in the kitchen cooking with her newly reacquainted friend who was an unstoppable talker. Nadia was once again to sense what it was that drew her to this place. Standing in Maria's kitchen with its familiar but exotic aromas of frying buckwheat and garlic, dill and flat leaf parsley, she could not help inhaling with it that nostalgic draw of the blood-tie of home. The smells, the wholesomeness, the very warmth of simplicity; these were what repeatedly drew her back.

Maria, it seemed, did not sleep. Long after we went to bed each night, she would be clearing up in the kitchen and we woke in the morning to hear her preparing tea and cooking breakfast. After the disaster of the village and the grim hospital stay and despite the relative comfort of the hotel, Maria's small flat was a perfect sanctuary. Though Lara was not permitted to sleep in Chemodanivka, the family was able to visit relations and granddad was able to come to Nedrighailiv.

***

Serendipitously, it was at Alyosha's house where Lara had been taken ill that the drama of the last day occurred. A final visit had been arranged to say goodbye and to collect gifts and souvenirs and of course Granddad. Valya had kindly driven the family to the village in his orange Lada estate car loaded with luggage. There was to be a long drive ahead in order to catch the train that would ultimately deliver us to Borispol airport in the capital. As ever with Ukrainian hospitality, we had been fed and were about to get in the car when we heard a vehicle approaching at some speed. The military jeep skidded round the bend in the lane next to the house and came to a sudden stop alongside us raising a cloud of choking dust.

Everyone was curious but no one was alarmed. It was the last morning, we were on our way home at long last and everything was in order. When the blue uniformed Olga Sergeyevna stepped out of the car, I immediately thought we must have forgotten something at the hotel and that she had kindly engaged the help of the policeman to get to us quickly to return it before we left. As I approached her, smiling in greeting, I was taken aback by the steely scowl on her face and the officious severity on that of the policeman. Family members seemed to shrink slightly out of deference in the presence of this state official.

The strident tone from the hotel manager was clearly accusatory. Shouting and pointing at the cases, she seemed to be insisting that they were to be opened for searching. Whilst family members were somewhat cowed, Maria, ever assertive, was furious.

"Why should they open the luggage?" she demanded hotly. "What on earth do you think they have? What could they want from you?"

Olga Sergeyevna was adamant that hotel crockery had been taken. She reported that on checking the inventory of the room after the visitors' departure, certain items that should have been there could not be found so obviously the foreigners must have them. Maria translated for our benefit.

"They are from the West," she shot at the hotel manager. "Don't you think they have these things in England? Why should they want your crockery? What is this nonsense?"

Nevertheless, watched by the clearly bored policeman, she insisted on searching the luggage and of course found nothing. It transpired later that she had failed to complete an initial inventory and was subsequently dismissed from her post.

***

Thus the girls did manage, albeit at a young age, to sample the land of their grandfather, the conditions in which he grew up and to experience intimately the difficulties of the developing USSR. They got to know and to love their wider family and they too, like their mother, came to absorb their own blood-ties with his roots.

The return journey home was less romantic or exotic than their arrival had been but they were delighted and relieved at last to be fast-forwarding once more.

More than once during the journey home Nadia expressed her emotional turmoil.

"That's the last time I ever come here. It tears me apart. Never again! It is just too hard. I'm not coming back ever."

But she did. The call to come back home never left her. In some primal way, she belonged. Like an unshakeable addiction, it did not take long for her to be drawn back. She kept returning as did the rest of the family. I returned to fulfil a promise to collect Ukrainian soil to place on the grave of Ivan Euphimovich. Nina returned to explore her family's roots for her MA final exhibition in fine art and Lara also returned to visit Maria and her family though she never again slept in the house that Alyosha built.

Nostalgia

Gazing at the photograph on his desk, he finds it hard to believe that he had taken it by chance. The slightly faded colour photograph appears carefully composed though it was in fact shot as an afterthought, in motion on the back of a horse drawn sled.

Clad in thick brown suede coat and brown fur hat, the eighty two year old man peers into shot from the right frame. He gazes into the middle distance across a snow-covered field. Over his shoulder a haystack about the size of a small dwelling stands in front of a line of spindly trees, the backcloth of the scene. All are covered in snow save for the contrasting dark of the branches and the man himself. There is no sign of modernity. The image is timeless.

His hazel eyes, tiny and sunk deeply into his weathered face, are usually inscrutable. In the photograph they are slightly squinted in protection against the bright low winter sunshine reflecting off the snow, but they are nevertheless preposessingly focused and gazing into the middle distance. Strongly expressive crows' feet wrinkles and the lines beneath the eyes betray a hard life lived.

He wears a full beard in the picture but the grey predominates. His chin is buried a little into the coat for warmth and his firm mouth is open enough to show his teeth. This is not a smile though; something more wistful than a smile: his expression speaks of nostalgia. He is unaware of the younger man beside him, out of shot, leaning back to take his photograph and he is also oblivious of the man driving the horse and sled. He is in this place transported to a far off time.

The background of the photograph is predominantly blurry white and with the dark tracery of the branches and the faded dun clothing, it could be an old monochrome image. It has a timeless quality linking the old man with the young boy in the field they share.

***

Though he had not been home in Ukraine during winter for almost fifty years, Ivan Euphimovich seemed to find it easy to walk on the treacherous surface, that slightly sideways waddle that allowed one to keep upright. It took the younger man a number of painful falls on the ice-hard snow before he almost got the hang of it. They had been in the village for around a week in late December. During that time there had been no snow but it was so cold that previous snowfalls had frozen and moving around was difficult.

On New Year's Eve, Ivan Euphimovich had excitedly insisted on a tour of friends and neighbours, remembering from his youth the traditional warmth, companionship and welcome that always occurred. There would be drinking and a great deal of singing, probably accompanied by accordion or guitars or even a balalaika. They took spirits and some gifts of food and after having visited a few neighbours' houses they found, disappointingly, that they had been tolerated rather than welcomed while usually the television set had been left playing. The one place where they found music was at the home of some young relatives who were dancing to loud western pop hits on the radio while smoking and drinking excessively. Times had changed and they had returned sadly before midnight to the house of his nephew, Alexei Trofimovich who himself was ill in bed with a weak heart.

Often the treacherous walk across the fields to the simple village shop might end in a tedious shivering wait, occasionally for several hours in minus ten degrees for the unreliable delivery. The errand was to purchase bread for the family. Very little else was ever available. No one seemed to be about; thoughts of community seemed to have ceased to exist. At these times the older man occasionally spoke and they reminisced about times when provision could be depended upon and the simple shop had been well stocked with beer to share as well as bread and other foodstuffs; when the local collective provided for most of the community's needs. For the most part, though, among his own people and mother tongue, Ivan Euphimovich usually kept his own counsel and the younger man had been largely ignored. The tedium, however, was to be soon lifted as an excursion had been arranged as a special mark of their winter visit.

With a clatter of hooves, the transport arrived in the lane outside the compound of Alexei Trofimovich's small brick cottage. The Brigadier had come as promised. He and the younger man had met fifteen years earlier at the collective farm where he was called the Brigadier because that had been his position in other times. After drinking and smoking together back then and clearly at ease in each other's company despite a lack of mutual language, the younger man gave his favourite slender churchwarden pipe to the Brigadier because he had clearly admired it greatly. The memory came back to him now but times had changed much during those years. Piotr Michaelevich, was still known as the Brigadier though now he was just the caretaker of the declining and dilapidated former collective farm buildings. Importantly he still had access to a horse and two-seat sled although there was no more collective farming and the land was being left to weeds. He had continued with his smoking habit but he was now forced by necessity to roll up coarse home grown tobacco in torn newspaper rectangles sealed with saliva. The years had taken their toll on him. Though still only around fifty, he was far too thin, coughed pitifully and was somewhat stooped. He was a skilled driver of horses, however, and he was the guide for the day.

Neither guest had any idea of what had been prepared for them on this special day out. Dressed in borrowed winter clothes of fur or suede coats and hats as well as thick boots, well protected against the freezing weather, they climbed into the back of the little sled with the old man on the right. Piotr Michaelevich groaned as he heaved himself onto the driver's bench behind the single horse and indicated with a curt click of his tongue for her to start the trip. Her hooves slipped in an alarming fashion on the slippery surface and it seemed for a while that she might spreadeagle painfully as she struggled to gain her footing. The roadway held little snow other than deeply frozen patches hardened into ice though the fields and surrounding trees were resplendent in virgin snow. It took little time for the horse to find her feet. Fortunately there was to be no further snowfalls that day and the winter sun hung low in a cloudless pale blue sky.

Though the horse had staggered worryingly at the start of the journey, she managed the rest of the terrain with ease and seemed to have no difficulty pulling the sled even when they left the flat open fields and began to climb gradually upwards towards a forest. The purpose of the trip remained a mystery as they entered woodland which was mixed with deciduous and coniferous trees. Some distance into the centre of the wood, the Brigadier had the horse come to a halt and he indicated to the guests that they should dismount from the sled. After what was a fairly rocky ride, it was a relief to stretch the back and that was what the younger man was doing as the others spoke briefly. Ivan Euphimovich then approached him.

"Get wood. Pick dry sticks. Break dead branches from tree." Not a man of many words.

The younger man wondered if in fact they had been brought to the forest to collect wood to take back. On his earlier visits to the village years ago he had seen the babushkas, the old women, going out with ropes and, bent double with the weight, carrying back prodigious faggots of fallen branches strung together on their shoulders, loads far heavier than he might have managed himself. He was not keen on that task. When some small branches had been collected and taken back to the Brigadier, though, it became clear that he was preparing a bonfire in a small clearing. When it was substantial enough, he lit it with matches and a little spirit. He then passed over a sharp knife along with instructions to go for a small green branch. This, it became clear, was to act as a skewer.

They were to have a picnic in the snow of roasted pig fat (*salo*) and black rye bread (*xlib*). The younger man had eaten these foods before but never in such circumstances. *Salo*, he had been informed, is the thick layer of fat that lies beneath the skin of the pig. A healthy pig has a good thick layer of tasty fat and it is a popular part of the diet of rural Ukraine, especially in winter for which it is stored.

The brigadier distributed small pieces of *salo* and hefty chunks of *xlib* that he had carved with his extremely sharp penknife. This nutty, tasty black bread is the staple of the country. He was shown how to skewer the s*alo* on the green stick and roast it in the flames until hot and then, holding the bread underneath to catch the melting juices, wait for it to cool a little before eating the delicious, hot porky fat and the juice enriched *Xlib*..

Ukrainians never eat without a drink, though, and this winter snowy barbeque in the forest was completed when Piotr Michaelevich produced a half-litre bottle of homemade vodka. Known locally as *khorilki,* it is both strong and delicious. When swallowed in one gulp, its fire and flavour can be felt as it flows down the throat, through the chest and into the stomach. They say you can feel the feet of Christ. Three *sto gram* (100ml) glasses also appeared and thus the companionable group was able to toast "peace", "friendship" and "life" with shots downed in one in the traditional way. *Salo, xlib* and *khorilki*. This elemental meal would have been enjoyed in winter snow by fire by generations of Ukrainian men. Some things never change and perhaps that was why this unusual meal in the snow, in the forest had been prepared for the visitors. This demonstration of traditional customs was a gift for them. It had been a privilege.

It was getting late in the afternoon and the forest, silent save for the crackling of the dying fire, the wind in the snow clad trees and the rattling halter of the horse was beginning to cast shadows. The temperature began to fall.

The memorable folkloric lunch came to an end and they had to return to the village before nightfall that settled early in midwinter. A little heady, they were happy to get back on the sled and the Brigadier had the horse set off as gently as possible.

Probably to save a little time the return was by a slightly different route. Descending from the forest, they drove across snow-covered fields that had once been farmed by the collective before falling into neglect after the collapse of the Soviet Union and the end of collectivism. Both guests were at first quietly contemplative on the journey home after their picnic in the snow, probably helped by the *khorilki* consumed.

Ivan Euphimovich had been silent for some time so the younger man turned to his right to check on him. All seemed well so he leaned out to his left to increase the distance for the shot and took a rushed photo for a souvenir. There appeared to be a slight break in the old man's normally taciturn demeanour and he seemed to be smiling wistfully, his mind elsewhere. He was staring eagerly into the middle distance. Was there perhaps a glimpse of a tear? His hazel eyes seemed fixed as if in deep thought. And then he spoke, a barely perceptible choke in his voice.

"You know what," he started, gesticulating with his right arm to indicate the field across which they were being driven. "I was little boy when I ploughed this field. This very field." Then he looked piercingly, rheumy eyes impossible to avoid and a tear clearly visible.

"I walked with plough behind ox. Was barefoot. Always was working. Long days and no shoes. Barefoot ploughing. Was really hard. Hard life. You know what, I was twelve and it was so hard; I was hungry but I would like to be there again; if only; to have that life again."

The young boy and the old man in the field that they share.

The Bear

Ours, I thought, was an unbreakable friendship. For twelve years we lived just three miles apart in Somerset but then we both moved. You left teaching early to take that shop in Taunton and I went to Exeter to be closer to my widowed father-in-law.

For me you were too important to let geographical distance get in the way. Instead of walking three miles, I drove thirty so we could continue to have our nights out. You never managed to get down to mine – until that evening in June when you both came for dinner.

***

I first met you in the lounge bar at the Crown Hotel. The four of us met at the suggestion of your wife who had become our daughters' piano teacher. We were new to the area and glad to have the opportunity of meeting new friends. That initial drink together was the first of many.

Fairly short and powerfully squat with a full dark beard, your trademark Palestinian keffiyeh round your shoulders, you held a cigar whose smoke curled around your head and your apparent self-assuredness gave the impression of a movie star. In your late thirties, you resembled a slimmer, younger Peter Ustinov, an impression reinforced when you spoke in greeting. Your mellifluous dark chocolate voice evidently served you well as a primary school head teacher and also on stage, drama being one of your passions. Your slightly Mediterranean complexion clearly derives from your Armenian heritage, your grandfather, you told me, having been driven out of Turkey in the pogroms of the early twentieth century.

The firmness of your initial handshake and the warmth in your dark eyes betrayed unquestioning self-confidence as well as a welcoming friendliness. That firm handshake was to develop between us into hugs, embraces, arms across the shoulder and sporting arm-wrestles as we grew to know each other over a dozen or so years. This physicality manifested itself in all sorts of ways including competing with each other in squash, running, walking and cycling together and on one occasion, much to your delight, your beating me in the local triathlon. Both teachers, we were also similar in so many other ways. Fairly equal in build, strength and fitness, we also had shared interests in so much including real ale.

I clearly remember a moment in the garden of the Black Smock on the Somerset levels. It was the sort of sunny afternoon that our memories often kid us that English summers are made of. We'd been for a long country walk to the bird sanctuary and were enjoying our well-earned refreshment in the sunny garden.

You bent down over your pint as it sat waiting for you on the table and you almost kissed it, "I love you beer." Typical of you, performative and passionate.

You and I were close. Tight. We'd even declared our love for each other. It was so real, so important. When together nothing was off the table. We discussed everything: education, ethics, music and drama, sport, politics, sex and relationships.

An ardent man, you craved passion from everyone, including your wife. You seemed used to getting your own way and you didn't like to be crossed. I noticed sometimes how you seemed discomfited in the company of strong women and you even expressed dislike for some of our female friends who stood up to you. That said though, you surprised me one day when you insisted on your strong belief that "fools *should* be suffered gladly". It had not occurred to me to challenge that old trope that we should admire those who "wouldn't suffer fools". The idea that intolerance of the failings of others could be seen as something to laud and celebrate was anathema to you. Not only did I love you for that sentiment but I have been guided by it ever since.

Though we frequently spent Saturday afternoons going to support Yeovil Town, as our local league side, you were a Liverpool fan for some reason and, born in the North East, I have always followed Sunderland. They had just been promoted to the Premier League after building a beautiful new stadium and everything seemed very positive for their future. Such was my pride and confidence that, muddle-headed with ale, I offered you a bet.

"I bet you a fiver that Sunderland will never be relegated again in my lifetime."

History records that they only lasted a couple of years before being relegated again and I duly paid up. In that drunken moment it hadn't occurred to me that even if I were to have won the bet, I would never have been able to collect. The things we did. The things we said.

I came to love you. I have never found such deep, fraternal physicality and mutual candour in any other male friend. A really precious thing.

***

Leaving the village, the dim street-lights are now behind us and we must depend on the pallour of a feeble cloud-covered moon to guide us as we stagger along the centre of the main road between our homes. Apart from the muffled rustle of spring leaves and gentle movement of cattle on the other side of the hedge, the night is quiet. By day the road is well used by speeding traffic but now, after midnight, the drivers are probably in bed asleep and we have the highway to ourselves. We have drunk too much to be overly concerned and we expect to be alerted by engine noise to any approaching vehicle. Arm in arm, brothers in arms, we strive to follow the white line though frequently the tilt and loss of balance of one or other of us steers both off course. Sensibly, you have left your car at home knowing we would have too many pints. This time you have been "playing away" at my local knowing you had a three mile walk home at the end of the night. Some times it goes the other way and I do the homeward journey on foot. It has been a good night and despite the differences between us and some awkwardly frank conversation, we are feeling good; so much so that I have decided to accompany you for most of your journey home before I will retrace my steps to my own village and my sleeping family.

"I love you, mate." I say and I mean it, reinforcing the words with a tighter squeeze of your shoulders.

"I love you too, Dave."

Then quiet. Trees sussurating in the spring night, the hazy moonlight guides us on our way and we stumble on in silence.

***

Yes it had been a good night. The usual three-pint argument kicked in again. We liked to talk politics and both hated the Tories but, ever the stubborn fucker, after three pints, you dug your social democrat heels in as usual and just couldn't accept my wider, more left-wing, internationalist view of imperialism. It didn't matter though. Nothing was off the table with us and tonight you clearly had other stuff to talk about. We had often discussed our marriages and occasionally mentioned our sex lives. I couldn't and wouldn't discuss these topics with other friends, even close mates, but there was something about the candour of our comradeship that made such confessional conversations not only normal but totally unthreatening. I felt I could share anything with you. What you asked me, though, stopped me dead.

"Have you ever had an affair or thought about it? Ever had eyes for someone else?"

"Not really," I stammered, caught entirely off guard. "No, well, not really. No. I mean…I might have had a fancy occasionally, like a flirtation. Like everyone, we've had our ups and downs but I've never really thought about propositioning anyone else. To be honest, mate, I've always reckoned on there being too much to lose." I looked at you quizzically unable to imagine what had brought this on. "That's apart from the fact that I'd be hurting someone I love. I mean, I don't think I could do that. We have talked about it and agreed that if we strayed that would be the end. We probably couldn't stay together. For me marriage is all about trust, isn't it, and once that trust is broken it can't be mended. Like a shattered crystal glass, it can't be put back together. Corny, I know, but that's how I have always felt. If either of us cheated there would be no going back. No rebuilding a damaged relationship. End of. Know what I mean? Then there's our daughters. I've always said that if we divorced, I couldn't face being a Saturday dad or a once in a fortnight Dad. If that ever happened I think I would almost rather say goodbye to my children for ever and I just don't think I could bear that; I could never lose them."

'*Our daughters' resonated with me as I said it because I had been struck on many previous occasions by how you always referred to 'my boys' and never 'our sons' as if your wife had nothing to do with them. You'd insist on how much "I love my boys" and how much more important to you than your wife were "my boys".*'

"That's the thing, see Dave. That's what I wanted to tell you." You dropped your head in your hands but continued to look up at me through your fingers. "You know that I was divorced from my first wife who left me for someone else." A hesitant pause before you continued, "but what I didn't tell you was that I had a daughter with her and I haven't seen her since. I last saw her when she was three so she would be around twenty now."

"You haven't seen your own child in seventeen years? Fuck, mate! That must be constantly tearing you up. How can you cope with that? Surely it is never too late to put that right. Do you hear anything about her? Do you want to? I mean, what about her? She must be curious about you."

"I guess I kind of became used to the idea that I don't have a daughter. I've got my boys and you know they are absolutely everything to me. It's true what they say about your ex turning your kids against you and I just reckon she was poisoned."

"There's been absolutely no contact at all? Mate. Jesus! I'm so sorry; that is total shit."

"Actually that isn't the whole truth. She did write me a letter a few years ago wondering about meeting up. I guess she must have been around seventeen at the time but I kind of never got round to making it happen. Somehow, too much had passed by. This was when a load of other crap was going on in my present marriage so dealing with that would have added too many complications. Affairs and stuff. That's why I asked you the question. All a bit of a mess when I think about it."

I was stuck for an answer so I left it hanging. "Other crap." That was news to me. I didn't know what you were referring to and I didn't know what to say. Our glasses were in need of a refill so I grabbed the chance to gather my thoughts.

"My round, mate. Jesus Christ. Same again? Back in a mo'."

I was glad of a pause in this heavy confessional. What could have made you come up with this now? As I went to the bar I was reeling from the impossibility of what I had just heard. My family life was by no means always a bed of roses and the girls could at times be a worry but I couldn't imagine the life you had had. But there was more to come.

"Yeah, affairs," you sighed as I sat down again with our two pints of Otter. "That corny crap you said about broken glasses. Did you mean all that? Don't you really think a marriage can't be repaired after infidelity? Ever? Really? I reckon mine was."

"Mate, didn't you just tell me that your marriage broke up in divorce and that you lost your daughter? That is pretty fucking comprehensive isn't it? Sorry, I mean, hurtful though it is and I wouldn't rake it up but that would seem definitive, mate." I was genuinely confused and had no idea what you meant but you soon put me straight.

"No, I mean my present marriage. Didn't you know?"

"Know what? What am I meant to know?" I asked, perplexed.

"Your bloody crystal glass, Dave. She broke it when she had an affair with some bloke she met in a pub where she was a barmaid a few years ago. I was on a Head's residential somewhere, I don't remember. Things had been a bit rocky around that time and while I was away she shagged somebody else."

"What? Of course I didn't fucking know. As far as I know she hasn't told my missus and that's the first time you've told me. That's just awful. How on earth did you both get over that? You know maybe I'm wrong about it. What do I know, mate? I've never been there. Sorry. Maybe it is possible to rebuild. Where does that leave you though with trust? Is it possible to ever trust someone who has betrayed you like that? Don't get me wrong, I'm not judging her. She is really lovely but she hurt you. How does that work?"

I reckon I was feeling a bit out of my depth here but digging myself deeper.
"Reciprocation, I suppose you could call it," you replied. "I've never really felt I wanted to have sex with anyone else particularly and I probably wouldn't have if that hadn't happened. Anyway, I found someone else. It was only casual, brief and fairly meaningless but I supposed that evened up the score and we've gone from there really. Not ideal but it seems to work." The glimmer of a sardonic smile flashed across your sad eyes.

You went out to the toilet at that point, giving me another chance to process what I was hearing. Enough ale had been drunk to fuddle my brain but all this was hard to take in or to know how to respond to.

'Affairs, That's "the other crap". Not ideal? Reciprocation. Seems to work? Too many complications? My boys.'

I was reeling after this intensity. How different your life has been to mine. How different you are to me. And how hurt. Betrayed twice, abandoned daughter and an adulterous wife. I was touched with the brutal honesty of your revelations, almost like you were baring your wounds. I felt like you had bestowed on me alone a fragile gift that I must value: your trust. And I loved you for it while at the same time questioning your actions. Or was I judging your values?

***

We met each other's parents. Mine really liked you, I recall, and you told me you had enjoyed my Dad's stories – and his single malt I expect. You were doing the Cleveland Way or some such and you were glad to take a break from camping rough by accepting a night's rest at their bungalow in Whitby. Mum told me later that you really enjoyed the full English breakfast she cooked for you but then you never let on that you are a committed vegetarian.

You met my Ukrainian father in law, Ivan, as well and I thought you seemed to get on pretty well at least superficially, your own East European heritage a connecting point though I have to say I was left with the feeling that you misread things a little. Like you, he was also a very proud man and, being considerably senior, he probably expected rather more deference than he was accorded by you. He was too polite to deride a friend of mine but I was left in no doubt that he didn't warm to you. He seemed to have seen in you what occasionally troubled me: that ego.

So you knew my parents and met my father-in-law but I didn't really get to know your folks at all though I did meet them twice during their rare visits. Straightforward working class people, they were getting old and were not in the best of health. Strangely, you seemed to tolerate them with some embarrassment rather than show much affection. I remember you telling me that you didn't feel close to them and in fact you even once admitted that you didn't actually like them very much. You hardly ever went to visit them though you told us proudly that your mum's face would light up whenever she saw you walk through the door. You were the light of her life. She was so proud of her headmaster son and she loved you so much. There is something universally profound and almost mystical about mothers and their affection for their boys. What had happened, I wonder, to cause you antipathy to your own family? You never alluded to it.

You said that luckily your sister lived close by and though she had her own family including her disabled child to look after, she did the caring for them, a role that so often falls to the daughter. It seemed a little strange to me that a man with such compassion for others, who asserted the need to "suffer fools" didn't seem to suffer his own wider family with much warmth or affection. How could one with such passion and warmth have so little for his birth family? When it came to the need, after their deaths, to do up their house for the market, you went there quickly and frequently though you never told me of any visits to your sister. Did you go to see her I wonder?

***

A few years elapsed during which I came over to stay with you a few times for a drinking session. Eventually we persuaded you both to come for dinner one evening in June.

Vegetarian of course. We were planning to eat and drink together and for you to stay over.

The visit did not go well.

Our lives had gone in different directions and the common ground had shrunk. Both of your folks had died in the intervening time and so had Nadia's dad. It was late in the evening after dinner and we had all drunk far too much. The alcohol-fueled lack of inhibition evident in the 'three pint argument' was magnified.

Nadia had always been a loving and loyal daughter. Her ingrained need to care for her parents was implacable. She couldn't understand your disdain for your late parents or indeed your abandonment of your lost daughter. She always understood why you were so important to me and how you filled what she saw as a need in me but she always found you stubborn and, dare I say it, somewhat arrogant. She is not just a strong woman but perceptive and ardent too and that ardour was burning in her that night. She was not going to rest until she had challenged you; until she had poked the bear.

"I'm really sorry to hear about your Mum and Dad," she began. "It must be hard for you. It takes some time to come to terms with. Are you feeling OK?"

"Well you probably know that I didn't feel too close to them," you replied, probably rather too dismissively. "Though I have to say that the inheritance has come in handy in helping us with our business."

"Inheritance? Do you mean they left you some money? Didn't you tell us your sister did all the caring?"

"Yeah, it was split two ways in the end. Two of us. Half and half."

"Really? Shouldn't you have let your sister have it? After all she also has a disabled son and didn't she do all the caring for your parents? You were never there and she was on their doorstep. Can that be right? You did nothing and you didn't even like them. Should you have the same as her?"

This was awkward because you knew that she could only have heard this from me and I was initially taken aback. I really wish she hadn't gone here.

"Look Nadia," you were reddening with anger. "That is out of order. This is none of your business and you have no right even to comment. In any case this money is not just about me; it's for my boys. I don't have to justify myself to you. You have no idea what my childhood was like; what I went through. What the hell do you know? I see this as recompense for the shit I had as a kid, for the lack of love. You don't know the half of it."

Never, in any of our exhaustive and deeply personal conversations had you ever mentioned any difficulties in your upbringing. It was getting too embarrassing and I wanted to intervene but there was no stopping her. These family loyalties were so much a part of her and though she later acknowledged she was at fault, the drink had got to her and she was on a roll. She had the reckless stubbornness and persistence of her father and wasn't going to be stopped.

"I'm sorry but at least you did have both of your parents as a child. You abandoned your own daughter at three didn't you? What kind of childhood did she have? You don't even know. You didn't even ask. You didn't want to know." I knew then that that was it. Again, she could have heard that only from me.

You stood up and growled, "I've had enough of this. Who the fuck do you think you are to judge me or my life? What on earth makes you think you have the right? That's it for me. Dave, you're welcome to come up to see me in Taunton but I'll tell you this: I'll never darken your bloody doorstep again."

Nadia tried to back track, "Look, I am so sorry. Me and my big mouth. You are right. It is not my place and it is not my business. I've had too much to drink. Please, I'm really sorry. Please sit down again. Please. I'm so sorry."

You were not for suffering anybody gladly then though and you went immediately to bed. The evening fizzled out in embarrassed silence. What a mess.

I found it hard to sleep after all the drama and when, hours later, I heard movement downstairs I went down and found you sitting in the gloom of the kitchen, still clearly upset, pouring a whisky. It was approaching the solstice and through the kitchen window a faint glimmer of light could be seen as dawn approached. I asked if you were ok for me to join you. Your beef was not with me you said, so I also had a scotch and we sat together.

Surely it couldn't end like this.

I thought I heard a nightingale and we took the bottle with us onto the terrace. It was nearly four and day was breaking. You might remember that miserable grey early morning when birdsong filled the gloomy air and a delicate soft drizzle settled gently on our heads and shoulders. I've never forgotten. My appeals for you to accept Nadia's apology fell on deaf ears. I tried so hard to mine our deep friendship for compassion, forgiveness or tolerance but got nowhere. The bear had been well poked. You had a sore head and a sorry heart but stubbornness reigned.

You surprised me with the words you said. That I took a while to realize their import is why I remember them verbatim.

"Dave, I really admire you. I'm in awe, mate. I have to say you are the strongest, toughest and hardest bloke I've ever known. I really admire your resilience and strength."

Clearly you had been preparing this little speech. These words were intended more as an attempted backhanded slight of Nadia than a genuine compliment to me but in fact they say more about you, my one time friend.

I knew I was seeing the end of a unique, profound and special friendship. I also knew that, though you invited me to come and visit, I could never see you again. Several whiskies and an hour or so later we parted with our last strong, sad, silent embrace.

In the morning, once again I tried to get you to accept Nadia's apology but you refused. Once again you offered to welcome me if I chose to come to see you in Taunton. Though I had tried hard to mediate, my loyalty was clear. Before you were taken home you repeated your strange assessment of me. "Resilience and strength"? Does it take such strength to love and respect a strong woman?

You drove off and I never saw you or spoke to you again.

Light Show in Addis

It was once again the light in Africa that had forced itself on my consciousness as we'd set off after dark on that Tuesday evening. On this occasion it was not that pellucid light of the African day but an irregular, intermittent and seemingly artificial light that flashed at night around the city. Ethereal and eerie, it was a whitish light that appeared now and again behind the high-rise buildings. It flashed spectacularly like sheet lightning, but unlike lightning it glowed at ground level rather than illuminating the sky's canopy. I dismissed the idea that it might be lightning since there was no accompanying thunder and I'm used to lightning that lights the whole sky. I assumed it must have been some kind of laser light show presented as part of the celebrations to commemorate the annual conference of the African Union that had been taking place at its headquarters in the capital during the week. It was certainly a show that would have impressed the visiting heads of state.

Throughout the week, soldiers in grey camouflage fatigues had been stationed throughout the main parts of the city on nearly every corner, most carrying automatic weapons. Occasional motorcades with police motorcycle outriders had sometimes delayed us in getting to work. Individual highly polished black Mercedes executive saloons, windows darkened, national flags fluttering on the bonnet had passed us on the streets and our infrequent glimpses of Ethiopian TV had shown a smiling Meles Zenawi, the Prime Minister, as he greeted and fraternized with African heads of state. The presence of Colonel Gadaffi and his entourage from Libya, a pariah in the West, had caused a flutter in the British ex-pat community so it was not only the local populace who had found excitement in the week-long event. Small wonder then that the city might have wanted to observe it all with some kind of light show though we both struggled to understand what kind of artifice could manufacture the kind of extraordinary, otherworldly periodic luminescence that we had been witnessing for over about half an hour. We took a line taxi to Mexico Square near the city centre where we needed to change route and it was only then that the meaning of the light show became clear.

The initial heavy raindrops falling on our heads warned us what we were in for. Just as we were well clear of the line taxi, wandering the street, unsure of our directions and desperately wondering how to find another to where we were going, it became clear that we were about to be caught in an Ethiopian rain storm and that we had been wrong about the light all along. I then realised that, given that Addis Ababa is over 2300 metres above sea level, the lightning must appear very differently here and that as relative newcomers, we had yet to experience it. I normally carried a pocket-sized folding umbrella but I had yet to use it. It could be said to be an essential piece of equipment here because although at that time of year it is almost always sunny and rain is extremely rare, when it does come it is usually sudden, unpredictable and it cascades in torrents, increasingly rapidly but usually decreasing as quickly. It is brief but potentially devastating to unprotected pedestrians. It was just our luck that for once I forgot it just as we were in danger of very quickly becoming soaked and when we really had very little idea of precisely where we were going or how to get there.

We were still some way off, trying to locate the appropriate line taxi and we were in imminent danger of getting totally drenched. Yet again we were faced with the dilemma of whether or not to pay the extortionate fare for a private taxi. This time expediency got the better of principle just as a battered blue and white car pulled up alongside us. We hesitated only briefly to negotiate a price to our destination and jumped in, relieved to be rescued from a certain soaking.

Taxis in Addis Ababa are uniformly cobalt blue and white ancient Soviet-built Lada saloon cars, leftovers from a previous era. Almost without fail they are dented, missing hubcaps, have holes in the radiator grille and cracks in the windscreen. They are smoky but mobile. As we accepted the ride in our cab, though, it was clearly in a far worse state than even the worst and oldest taxi I had seen in the city. At that time, Mexico Square was crowded with animated wet commuters in a deluge, desperate to get somewhere. Every available taxi was commandeered in an instant and we were uncertain what we might do when the ancient cab pulled up beside us. Its driver, spying well-dressed foreigners, was hoping for an inflated fare. Caught in a tropical storm without coat or umbrella, we were fairly desperate and relieved to jump in hoping for the best. But the external appearance of this jalopy did not forewarn us of just how dangerously un-roadworthy it was.

It was impossible for anyone to drive in these conditions. I was afraid for my life. The splintering headlights through the unwiped windscreen presented an incomprehensible aura, a kaleidoscope of dancing sparks through rapidly moving mass. The rain was intensifying and visibility was becoming a problem, exacerbated by the fact that the windscreen wipers were barely moving. Peering desperately out onto the road from my place beside the taxi driver, I was terrified. I could only see a vague suggestion of what was dense Tuesday evening city centre rush-hour traffic; pixilated approaching headlights in the dark, moving metal mass, silhouetted shapes of drenched pedestrians and endless torrential rain. As each blade crawled across it every few seconds the windscreen was still left smeared and bleary.

Even inside the car we were getting wet since none of the windows could be fully closed. I had to sit very close to the driver and Nadia was sitting loose in the middle of the back seat. We didn't speak. We were concentrating hard, paralysed with fear. Had we wanted to use the seatbelts, unusual in Addis Ababa, it would not have been possible as they were also not working. The malfunctioning wipers might have had something to do with the car's electrical circuit because it was clear that none of the lights were working either. We were in an ancient leaking taxi with bald tyres, malfunctioning windscreen wipers and no headlights driving through the worst torrential storm we had ever experienced in thick traffic on an unlit city-centre road during the rush hour. It got worse.

I struggled to see anything on the road other than this kaleidoscope of shapes and fractured lights in a monsoon. I prayed that we were traveling slower than it felt like because it just seemed impossible to avoid an eventual collision. Notwithstanding our terror, we admired the ability of the driver who somehow managed to swerve to miss buses and line-taxis and avoided potholes as he skilfully negotiated the rough terrain of incomplete and unmarked road works all the while seemingly driving blind through the dark torrent of the ferocious storm on bald tyres through the river that was flowing down the tarmac. The engine stalled and took some time to restart causing the windows to mist up immediately so it was even more difficult to see what was going on outside. I began to worry about our situation more intensely as the light show became a glowing smear.

The driver grinned as he spoke to us, "Fuel good. *Ishe*." Meanwhile he was frantically trying to clear the windscreen of condensation.

"Well done," we replied, trying to praise him for his skill while desperately holding our nerves. The car briefly stalled a second time but it was the third that was final. We were stuck.

We had actually passed our destination when the ancient machine terminally ground to a halt. Though it was still raining steadily the worst of the downpour was over and the thickest traffic had been left behind. We found ourselves on a fast, unlit dual carriageway in the suburbs crawling past our destination that was situated on the opposite side of the road. There was no gap through which to make a U-turn or obvious place where a pedestrian might have been able to cross. Both sides of the carriageway were fenced in by continuous waist high steel barriers and adjacent to our road to the right there was a minor road. At this point we were going downhill steadily and, as is the habit of all Addis taxi drivers, our man turned off the engine to freewheel thus saving fuel – in the rain with no lights and having already stalled twice! Any superfluous distance cuts into profit and after about a mile past the destination he was becoming exasperated with finding nowhere to turn round. At that point the ancient relic ground to a halt and finally expired. The driver leapt out leaving his door open, called "Fuel!" over his shoulder and went to the boot. He grabbed a jerry can before heading across the dual carriageway towards a Shell petrol station. Even through the rainy night I could see it was closed.

It was still raining. It was dark. The defunct taxi was stranded with driver's door open, mid-lane on a fast and busy unlit road without rear lights. We were inside and there seemed to be no refuge outside. Then we realized that Nadia was trapped in the back as we saw that both rear door inner handles were missing. Though hanging from the door, my handle thankfully did work so I got out intending to check whether at least the side-lights were on. From the rear of the car, I saw clearly that there was very little chance that any vehicle approaching at speed would see us in time. The storm had passed but it was still raining slightly and I was getting wet so I didn't want to suggest that Nadia should come out as well but that was what she was actually trying to do. In any case, with the fairly high fences it was going to be difficult to escape from the carriageway. I was really unsure of the safest course of action and was about to advise her to lie across the back seat to minimize any risk of injury just as the car was hit a glancing blow on the rear wing by a mini-bus line taxi and shunted several feet. The impact was not great but there was a sickening scrape as the already badly dented line taxi detached itself and went on its way, the young conductor (*wayalla*) simply poking his torso through the side window to check out the cause of the impact.

This was the point at which we decided to abandon our wreck to its fate and, during a lull in the traffic, I released Nadia through the nearside door. Sadly our taxi driver was having a bad night. He had had his car bashed and he lost his fare. Generous as ever, Nadia was clearly concerned for him but any pity I might have felt was more than counterbalanced by the fact that he had been willing to risk our lives in his un-roadworthy wreck.

Just beside where we had ground to a halt, on the opposite side of the minor road running to our right, we saw the lights of a tiny souk and a bar and the noise of the impact had attracted the attention of some young men who came to our aid. They helped Nadia to clamber across the barrier and offered to drive us back up to our destination – at a price. By this time we were in no mood for haggling so we agreed a price broadly equivalent to what we would have paid the taxi driver, climbed into their ancient saloon and finally arrived, a little shaken but not too wet, at Addis Ababa Golf Club where we were to enjoy an eagerly anticipated evening with the celebrated Senegalese musician, Baaba Maal. By the time we emerged from the old car the rain had stopped. Things were at last looking up and the young men who had rescued us, whilst no Samaritans, drove off with some easily earned cash. They had been as lucky as our taxi driver had been unlucky.

Though the Golf Club was fairly inaccessible by public transport and it was a mid-week gig, we were excited. Seeing one of Africa's most respected performing artists in the city that was the home of the African Union in the very week of its annual conference was going to be special. Tickets were really expensive. I had mentioned this three days earlier to the friendly young woman at the ticket office and I asked where on earth the audience might come from if local people couldn't afford it. She was confident that with the AU conference in town there wouldn't be a problem and she anticipated a great night.

We had heard that the golf club had a good restaurant so we had factored in time to have dinner before the concert was due to start at around ten. In spite of our adventure in the storm we arrived with ample time to eat though by then we were more in need of a drink than food. As we entered the lobby of this exclusive and expensive venue a female voice called out.

"Nadia! Nadia! So glad you could make it. Hi."

I was surprised to hear Nadia greeted by name and I looked round to see her being embraced, as if by an old friend, by a stunningly beautiful young Ethiopian woman. Nadia was equally nonplussed as she did not recognize her and therefore took her to be a student from one of the classes at her college. She also addressed me by name and it transpired that it was the friendly young person who had sold us the tickets for the concert. It seemed strange that she should remember the names of individual customers and it made us wonder just how few tickets must have been sold unless she just had a prodigious memory. Unexpected though it was, I still enjoyed the warmth of this lovely greeting and I took the opportunity to ask about the specific venue.

"Look, I can see that this is just a Golf Club," I asked, "so where will the concert be? Is there a large hall here somewhere? What kind of size audience are you expecting? Did you sell many tickets in the end? It seems very quiet. Where is everybody?"

"Oh, David, it is an outside event," she replied with a smile but no suggestion of irony.

Shaking the rain drops from my jacket, I asked in disbelief, "Come on, you are joking, right? In this weather?"

"No! Seriously, you should see the amazing set we have. The sound system is amazing too and we have the most wonderful light show to go with the music. It is early yet and the show will go on 'til three or four am. You will love it. You can see that the rain has now stopped and everything will be fine. *Ishe*."

Ishe: that lovely adaptable Amharic expression, loosely translated as *OK*, means everything is fine.

We had serious doubts about what she said but we settled for our meal and hoped for the best. Our concern about low sales continued though as there seemed to be relatively few people about. We speculated that, maybe, unknown to us, loads of people might be outside and that we really ought to go and check it out. We enjoyed our meal and, at around ten fifteen, we decided to venture out to see if the crowds had arrived and gone directly to the performance area without coming into the club.

As we stepped outside a distressing scene met our eyes. The vast stage and dark towering banks of speakers, now covered in plastic sheeting, were indeed impressive and a great deal of effort and expense had gone into the preparation but there was hardly anybody there. The sparse light from the few bare bulbs outside reflected sadly in the puddled water on the stage and sparkled on the droplets falling from the overhead cables. We were not surprised when we met the organizer of the event that he apologized profusely that the concert had been cancelled owing to the weather and that we would be entitled to a complete refund. I hoped for his sake that he had taken out sufficient insurance. Enormous expense had been incurred: colourful flyers and posters had been distributed, albeit at late notice, a stage set had been built with barriers and signs that would have graced any European outdoor festival and all for an event that was in the wrong place at the wrong time, overpriced and overambitious.

We discovered later, moreover, that Baaba Maal had given a concert on the previous evening at the ostentatious Sheraton Hotel exclusively for the visiting African Union heads of state and their entourages and that it had been broadcast live on state TV.

Death in Harar

"Drink Coca Cola".

Splashed in blood red paint across a white clay wall of a tiny souk opposite the hotel, it seems like vandalism or an act of violence especially incongruous here, right next to Harar's ancient Arabic wall with its triangular crenulations.

Belayneh Hotel sits beside the old city wall by Showa Gate. Between it and the wall is the chat market where around fifty or more women begin to pack away their unsold produce, ready to mix it with tomorrow's fresh consignment. Discarded leaves carpet the ground providing the local goats with a special supper. The end of the day at a busy marketplace: rubbish and the vendors' flimsy plastic bags blowing in the dust.

Harar is a noisy place, incessantly lively. Lorries belching blackness crawl up and down the streets laden with cattle, crops and goods for export to Djibouti and for transportation to other cities in Ethiopia. Ancient Peugeot 404 taxis from the sixties painted, like the Addis Ababa Ladas, in cobalt blue and white seem to prowl the city. Little three wheeled tuk-tuks in the same colours also tick noisily up and down the streets, a rhythmical background to the calling, shouting and persistent groan of traffic. To one side of the hotel is a loading point for goats and cattle destined for slaughter being placed into the Isuzu trucks. The trucks are nicknamed *Al Qaedas* owing to the suicidal risks taken by their drivers chewing chat during their night drive to Addis Ababa or other distant locations. Children call across the street, "Hyena! Hyena!" hoping to be recruited as guides for the famous Harar tourist attraction of hyena feeding. The night is noisy but the morning is noisier.

The concert begins at 4.45 am. Sunday morning is blessed by both the call to prayer from the Orthodox priest and from the muezzin. The chanting is sacred and soulful and it is so impressive that I rise to open the door to the tiny balcony in order to embrace the prayer-like invocations. The rich chocolate scent of roasting coffee fills the morning air while smoke from cooking fires thickens the blanket of mist lying across the roofs of the city in the pre-dawn light. The muezzin's voice loud and soulful, he calls the faithful to their first prayers. The Orthodox priests provide a deep bass-baritone as a steady ground, rising and falling in volume. Whilst the bass line continues, the muezzin is only permitted to call for a few minutes. After a brief pause, though, another mosque joins the music and a new muezzin in a different key enhances the melody. This is a holy moment. Harar's old city possesses nearly ninety mosques in a one square kilometre area though only eight have amplified prayer calls. It is sufficient. The lone early cockerel has no chance as he vainly tries to join the music.

A group of chanting young men approaching down the lane add to the chorus though they are more likely to be exuberant after a night's chewing than going gleefully to pray. The sounds of secular activity begin. A truck stops with a loud hiss of brakes, goats bleat and people shout. In time the prayer calls and Orthodox chants are only faintly audible, the street now full of the sounds of tuk-tuks tucking, voices calling, vehicles tooting, crates and cases crashing, animals bleating and children. Harar has come awake.

The hotel has also awakened. I can hear the noises of the staff from the kitchen and the smells of the breakfast and coffee preparing below sidle up to our floor. Two impassioned voices are raised in a nearby room. Hard to tell whether the language is Amharic or Oromaya but it is clear that the man and woman are unhappy. They try to keep the volume down, initially aware of the early hour and that others might still be asleep. Passions are running high, though, and their voices become steadily louder. Suddenly there is a startling crash like a falling wardrobe accompanied by shouting. More slamming follows with anguished screams. The sound of violence. For one man in the near vicinity, this is to be his last awakening.

***

Passing through the near desert scrub in the heat of the Awash basin and heading for the lush green of Chercher Mountains on the way to the ancient Muslim city of Harar, the only suggestion of any violence and bloodshed is the road kill of hyena, sheep and dogs and the presence of local Afar men guarding their huge flocks of cattle with rifles over their shoulders. The traffic travels fast at night, the drivers often stimulated by chat chewing. Accidents are common.

Dropping from the chilly heights of Addis Ababa, through the heat of the Awash region, then to climb into the verdant mountains before Harar, a road journey of around eleven or twelve hours, gives a good indication of the huge range of spectacular landscape that is Ethiopia. The Awash National Park is arid and at such times few animals could be seen. It is a Saturday and many local markets take place, each one providing much excitement and a splash of every bright colour. This is a very profitable growing country. Maize abounds and the region is famous for its excellent coffee but the most important cash crop is chat and there are fields of carefully planted rows of these bushes with their glossy leaves.

Just before Harar is Awadaye, the centre of the chat industry in this area. Most of the local crop is exported to Djibouti and the huge expansion of new building in the town is apparently being financed by chat which is chewed by people of both sexes and all ages in this part of Ethiopia, more so than in other parts. It is an activity that appears to be a community obsession and, particularly in the afternoon, many men seem totally inert whilst they sit or lie around, usually on the floor, chewing endlessly. The sight of people carrying handfuls of bunches of shiny green leaves is common in the area just before nightfall.

Harar comprises an ancient walled town inside a more modern city. The western approach is an impressive, tree-lined dual boulevard, illuminated by spirals of globe street-lights leading directly to the old city wall. Moorish and Egyptian influence is evident in the architecture long before arriving at the old town.

***

Sunday began with a guided tour of the market places of the new town. The markets were impressive despite the filth covering the ground. Every conceivable used and sometimes rusted metal object was on sale in the recycling market. Bedsteads, wheel rims, water tanks and chains were scarcely distinguishable from the corrugated zinc of the walls of the yard where they hung. The smuggler's market was the place to buy cheap contraband brought in illegally from Somalia. The draper was only distinguishable from her exquisite palette of colourful cloths because her face appeared between the folds and there was woman selling the most delicate injera made partly with sorghum.

As we continued our tour to the walled city I struggled to process the meaning of the raised voices I had heard in the hotel. If it had been a lovers' quarrel it was certainly passionate and I just hoped fervently that no-one had been seriously harmed despite the sounds of violence. The old city of Harar was teeming. We walked endless narrow streets where we had to step aside often for the passage of donkeys laden with contraband newly arrived from Somalia accompanied by men armed with Kalashnikovs, faces wrapped in shawls. The sense of criminality and violence stalked the city like a rumour. Camel meat was on sale, carcasses hanging bloodily outside the butchers' shacks and chat was available everywhere. On many streets there were groups of men lounging and chewing. We were surprised to come across and visit the house where the French poet Rimbaud had lived. Most of the low mud walled houses had been freshly if thinly washed in white or pastel distemper for the one thousandth anniversary of Harar due to take place in July that year. The walled city is dense and in places, suffocatingly congested with most of the streets being only a couple of metres wide. The narrowest of these lanes narrows to about a metre across. It is necessary to squeeze past anyone you meet and it is said in the town that you cannot meet someone, even an enemy, in this street without having to speak to them. It is called Reconciliation Street and it brought to mind the troubled couple in the hotel. Did they resolve their issues, I wondered.

On returning to the Belayneh I was surprised to see what looked like some kind of demonstration or melee outside and I also noticed that there were several armed policemen. The entrance was cordoned off and at first I was not permitted to enter. I was told that there had been some kind of lovers' fight and that no-one could enter. Whether different rules apply to western visitors or my entreaties were irresistible I'm not sure but I finally managed to gain permission to take our bag to the room though I was told to walk only on the side of the staircase furthest from the wall. As I crossed the lobby and approached the stairs I could see why. All the way down the stone stairwell up to around a metre above the steps the walls were smeared with blood. It was clear where someone's bloody hand had tried to get a purchase while seeming to have crawled or slid down the stairs bleeding profusely. Blood had also dripped to the landing where it had formed a large congealing puddle. Approaching our room I could see browning bloody footsteps coming from an adjacent room where the bed had been placed on its side as a barrier to prevent entry. I dumped our bag and returned to the lobby, astonished at having been allowed to enter what looked like a crime scene.

A young man had shot his lover and then himself. She had been wounded in the arm and had survived, crawling down the stairs for help but the man was dead. The couple were unmarried lovers who had often met in the hotel. He worked at the nearby hydro-electric plant. This was all we could find out. What makes a man take a gun to a tryst?

***

That evening outside the hotel, the light fading, the chat market is still busy. All around the bustling market square women are walking carrying oil, bowls, wood or sacks on their heads, frequently unaided by a hand. The tuk-tuks are still tucking and their drivers are clutching bundles of leaves. At the close of the evening, they sound like cicadas on chat. Again, despite the fading light, the rich colours of the Muslim women's shawls, cloaks and niqabs stand out in the gloom. A man walks past the hotel entrance carrying on his head a sliced off bottle green roof of a lorry's cab. Again the air is full of the sound of human voices calling, shouting, chatting and the endless drone of traffic against the bleating of goats. Below the hotel window the curious stop and stare, perplexed, at the room where but a few hours earlier a poor tormented soul had shot at his lover and killed himself.

A Patch Of Grass

You were absent for my birth: I was absent for your death.
From the outset your life is framed by hardship and conflict. Sent fatherless from your Anglesey village aged eleven to a charity boys' boarding school in Suffolk speaking no English, you learn to stand your ground. Four years later you are embroiled in the war in the Atlantic as a fifteen-year-old boy-sailor.

A shared moment provides a small window into your life as a teenager. We had come to the Fleet Air Arm Museum in Yeovilton with Mum on a rainy day when you were both visiting us in Somerset. You were well into your seventies and I was at a loss to know where to take you. By now I had children of my own and with your advancing years you had mastered your jealousy and aggression so we had put our personal war behind us. The suspended warplanes, displays of uniforms and endless charts of casualties were failing to maintain my interest so I just trudged on until I realized you were not by my side. Turning round to look for you I noticed that you were standing by a scale model of a ship. Roughly two metres long, it had your full attention. I joined you and saw that it was an aircraft carrier.

"The Ark Royal," you said. "I told you before about my time on her, about the hunt for the Bismark in the South Atlantic and about how we were torpedoed and sank off Gibraltar. Bloody hell, this brings it all back. See that little gun emplacement there, just on the starboard side amidships below the flight deck?" You pointed to a large anti-aircraft gun with a group of men around it before continuing. "I was just sixteen and I was the captain's boy. Sometimes I just held his heavy telescope and other times I had to run errands. That gun was where I was running to on one occasion with a message from the captain. We were under fire from German planes and I'd just come out from that hatch, there." You indicated a little doorway that would have been roughly thirty odd feet to the stern of the gun position. "I saw them take a direct hit. A piece of shrapnel just missed my ear but they had no chance. Instant explosion and nothing left."

You broke off and I turned to you to see if you were all right. I struggle to recall many occasions that I ever saw tears in your eyes. You had frequently entertained us all during family gatherings with repeated stories, often hilarious and sometimes harrowing, of your earlier life: nearly blowing your head off with a shotgun as a child, frequent scrapes with senior officers in the Navy, blowing the windows out of Scarborough sea-front houses and being depth charged as an experiment. This one, though, was visceral. You were living it again: your sixteen-year-old self sixty years earlier. A life forged in the heat of war is bound to be marked with violence and conflict.

***

ROUND ONE   Valletta, Malta 1950

Mum told me that we first met, not on a patch of grass, but on Valletta Harbour Steps. Posted to Malta, you were unable to attend the birth of your firstborn. You had lost the first battle over my name as she refused to call me Dafydd. She also remonstrated when you referred to me in a letter home as "little Dave". To Mum, I am David. It had taken us days to sail to join you for your two and a half year posting. I have no memory of my six-month-old self meeting his dad for the first time and seeing the bruises and black eyes on your face but Mum told me often that she found you in a sorry state. You tried to pass off a story that you had been injured playing football but she soon found out that you had been locked up for affray and only released that morning because of our impending arrival. Our stay in Malta lasted only six months as your confrontational and rowdy behaviour had us sent home early, you with a disrating.

You lose.

ROUND TWO   South Hylton, Sunderland 1953

Our ring is a patch of grass but more of a wasteland with rough weeds that reach up to our knees. My brother, John, and I are holding onto each other in what could be seen as a confused

dance. We are tiny. I am three and he is two. We are naked from the waist up and wearing long baggy cotton shorts that hang over our knees. We are barefooted and our hands are enclosed in heavy, primitive, junior sized leather boxing gloves that you have laced tightly around our wrists. You are teaching us to fight because you want us to be men. Like so many fighters, we learn that clinging on is less painful than being hit. In any case, we have no desire to hit each other, even to please our overbearing dad. We don't want to fight. So we stand there in a hapless cuddle. It is a warm sunny afternoon and I hold my arm around my brother's shoulder and smile in confusion while he looks down at his gloved hands wondering what he is supposed to do.
No contest.

ROUND THREE   South Hylton, Sunderland 1953
Realising that we are not keen to fight each other, you assume the role of sparring partner on the same patch of grass. You take John's pair of boxing gloves and balance them on the three middle fingers of each hand, drop to your knees and take your guard.
"Dukes up," you exclaim and demand that I take a similar guard with my right glove in front of my face and my left prepared to strike.
"Every time you hit my nose, I'll give you a sixpence."
Try as I might, your defence is too good for me but you refrain from attack.
Draw.

ROUND FOUR   Cubbington, Warwickshire 1965-68
You have driven home drunk again. We often watch through the front room window for the car returning in the evening, dreading what state you will be in. The way you stagger from the car tells us what is in store. Often you seem hardly able to stand and we know that there will be trouble ahead and that you will pick fights. The aggression is never physical but you are so ready to find fault and as a cocksure adolescent I am prepared to meet you head on. We often argue and with your alcohol-addled brain your last recourse is the offer to sort it out on the patch of

grass; the man's way. That patch of grass; your idea of parenting. I decline every time.
No contest.

ROUND FIVE   Cubbington, Warwickshire 1968
"Come on out the back," you bark again. "We can sort this out if you think you are so clever, so tough. There's a patch of grass. Just you and me. Man to man. Let's sort it out once and for all."

At eighteen I decide not to decline. Once again you can scarcely stand and can hardly speak. This time I have not been guilty of goading you or encouraging your rage. It is early evening and you are determined to cause a scene. For years this nonsense about the "patch of grass; mano a mano" has been a theme tune for my youth and I have had enough of it. I have decided to teach you a lesson.

"OK then," I reply when offered out. "Let's go and get it done. Come on. Outside. Patch of grass it is." I'm fed up with all this bravado and I move toward the back door. "Let's do it. Let's see what you've got."

"No David, stop it. What are you doing?" Mum tries to intervene pressing her hands to my chest but I reassure her quietly that no one will get hurt and gently hold her shoulders as I step to one side. I have no intention of fighting but I am curious to push it further in the hope of lancing the boil.

You find it difficult to stand still, swaying from side to side but you are growling and glaring into my eyes with fury, gamely prepared to see it through. You are breathing hard and are badly out of condition but I am puny at eighteen and I know that you can still hurt me if you decide to strike. This is high risk and I am afraid.

"Cummon," you grunt through grinding teeth, "hit me then. You can knock me over and then when I get up, it'll be my turn and I'll bloody well knock you over. Come on. Try and hit me."

"Dad, you asked me out here. This is your fight, your patch of grass so it is up to you to start it. You have to go first."

Given that you are so drunk I don't expect you to be able to hit me but deep down I know that you just can't. For all your big words I know that it isn't in your nature and that you are not able to strike me. I am hoping I am right. The futility and silliness of all this posturing is what I am hoping to get through to you and it seems to be showing signs of working. The hesitation is telling and your face shows signs of embarrassment. Maybe the drink is wearing off slightly or maybe the stupidity of this stand-off is getting through to you.

"You just can't do it Dad, can you?"

The sudden blow comes from no-where and my nose seems to shatter, my eyes blur and, as I raise them to my face, my hands are soaked in a cascade of my own blood.

John could have had no way of knowing what I was trying to do when he came home from the pub, walked into the sitting room and asked Mum where we were. He didn't wait to ask any further questions but came right out onto our patch of grass, grabbed my shirt and dropped his head onto my nose to stop me from hurting you. That was one of only two head butts I have endured in my lifetime and it hurt. I ran crying to the bathroom in pain to try to tidy myself up.

Bout abandoned

ROUND SIX   Cubbington, Warwickshire Christmas 1968

In retrospect I can see that I was at times a very difficult and challenging adolescent. You found me hard to cope with.

"David, you might be clever and know long words but you have no common sense and no personality," you said to me on a number of occasions. You knew where to strike.

In contrast to your own desperately difficult youth, my life was soft and unchallenging. In your eyes I had everything and gave nothing. Before his early death your father was a bully and you had no template for parenting, Raising three teenagers was so hard for you but I was the biggest challenge.

"Bloody kids! Maltese breaststroke, that's all it ever is," was another of your favourite expressions, often accompanied by a gesture with your arms that indicated taking everything in a grasping movement like hugging a large ball.

We have laid the "patch of grass" to rest but the conflict hasn't ended. This is the culmination of yet another contretemps between us and as it is coming to a head I begin to understand that I am at fault and I try to bring it to a close. You are furious and have got to the point of exasperation so you have the sense to walk away from me. I am angry with myself and am still trying to engage with you as I follow you to the stairs. You are half-way upstairs when you hear me, right behind you, muttering under my breath.

"You bloody fool….."

The blow to my left cheek as you turn and strike knocks me tumbling to the foot of the stairs and I don't stop at the door but open it and keep going.

You aren't to know that I am berating myself, not you. I explain it to you over a pint some time later. Notwithstanding this catalogue of macho posturing, this is the only time in my life that you ever touch me in anger.

Knock out win.

ROUND SEVEN   Newton Abbot, Devon Christmas 1976

This is our first married Christmas and, confused as to whose parents we should have, we decided to invite you all. You are all very different. On hearing his back-story, you acknowledged to Ivan, my father-in-law that you are both "peasants". He liked that and agreed. You are both exiles from your motherlands, both were born in rural poverty and have known real hunger. You each experienced unimaginable things in war and both have had to learn new languages. Neither of you were the recipients of much parental love as children. You have these things in common though very little else. Lacking a model of expressing your love, you engage me in a rugby scrum.

We have a plastic pitch this time, the kitchen vinyl floor a substitute for our patch of grass. Your left shoulder to my left shoulder, we crouch, struggling to get a purchase with our socks sliding on the pitch. Your tight-head prop to my hooker, we are simulating a scrum. This time we have both been drinking but it is Christmas day and we have had an excellent dinner. Our heads are touching and you are grinning and grunting heavily, grinding your teeth, as you push against me, your arms embracing my chest through play and physicality. At twenty-six, I play regularly as hooker in the local club but you still want to challenge me. At fifty-two, your playing days are long gone. I am also grunting, groaning, sliding and perspiring as I embrace you. There is love in this clinch but I dread where it might lead. For now it is harmless play.

We slide noisily around our large vinyl-floored kitchen looking and sounding like two wrestlers. On hearing combat, Ivan runs through from the dining room, asks no questions but immediately intervenes and wrenches us apart, sending me sprawling across the floor in order to protect you. Both mothers follow him into the kitchen and, seeing the melee, are thoroughly distraught. When we try to explain the purpose of our grunting embrace there is little sympathy from the assembled grown-ups in the room and voices and tempers are further raised. This is the last time we host Christmas for both families simultaneously.

Ivan wanted to be the ref but didn't know the rules.

No side.

LAST ROUND – CODA Windhoek, Namibia October 2008

This ground floor apartment is like a cave and admits little light, even in the increasing sunshine of late sub-tropical morning. While the tiny patch of grass seen through sliding doors at the end of the room is parched white from the sun, inside it is gloomy and chilly. This is exacerbated by the dark granite work surfaces and cold floor. I am alone, waiting to return home to England. I am desperate to see you one more time but I have hours to wait before taking the midnight flight; too much time to relive all these memories.

The rest of the family is around your bedside in Scarborough Hospital. I'm the only one missing and you are asking for me. I know that I have said everything that needs to be said. I wrote you that letter years earlier to express my love, respect and gratitude to you including for your war service. When we last met I promised you at your hospital bedside that I would look after mum. We have made our peace long ago. You know that I love you and I know that you are proud of what I have become. What more needs saying?

I am here in Africa with your blessing and approval though we knew this might happen. By the time of your heart failure diagnosis, Nadia and I had already been accepted for a posting in Namibia but the time never seemed right to break it to you. When we did tell you both, Mum was distraught.

In contrast, you paused thoughtfully before saying, "Well, that is something. You'll have to give me time to let that sink in." It was hardly a moment though, before you added, "That is amazing what you are doing. I'm really proud of you both. To leave home and your good jobs to volunteer to help poor people in another country; what a thing to do! Well done to you both. You musn't worry about us; we'll get by."

I am here alone, desperately hoping to get to you in time. Our Dilys called me yesterday when I was two hundred and sixty miles away in Tsumeb on a training course to let me know that the doctors said you had little time left. I was driven back to the capital into the night by colleagues in order to catch the first available flight. They have left me to make arrangements and to pack. They have borne my tales and my tears on the road and have offered comfort but I have to face the rest alone. Time is mocking me.

My phone rings in the middle of the afternoon. I am exhausted by thinking of you and crying.

I press *receive* and John's voice says quietly, "I'm sorry David but …."

Though not unexpected, that final blow is so painful and I howl.

Afrikaners

The huge Namibian Afrikaner was more than twice my size and I was more than scared but I just could not ignore what I had just witnessed. That's why, furious, I ran across the beach to confront him. I was beyond caution.

"What the fuck do you think you are doing? You could have murdered those children then. You never even gave them a chance to get out of the way. I saw you accelerate that boat right into them!"

My head came just up to the chest of his denim bib and brace dungarees but he was not expecting any one to challenge him so he was taken aback by my paroxysm of rage as I glowered up at his heavily bearded face. I sensed that he was slightly embarrassed to have been caught out deliberately driving his boat at the kids and he hesitated before muttering his feeble excuse. There were people a hundred yards or so across the water on the official swimming beach but they seemed oblivious to what I'd seen. The kids he nearly killed did not wait to see the outcome of this row.

"They shouldn't be there."

"What? In the water? Where should they be swimming? Is that an excuse to plough into them without warning? You fucking well saw them for Christ's sake!"

"On the proper beach, on the other side. That's where they belong. In their place."

"But you saw them. You drove straight at them!"

He then ignored me, turned his back and shrugged.

This confrontation took place on the boat-mooring beach at The Mole in Swakopmund just behind the sea wall. The afternoon sun was lowering over the Atlantic when the cabin cruiser bristling with deep sea rods and carrying three large-set, bearded white Namibians cruised sedately round the harbour wall, tacked to starboard abreast of the leisure beach and sped towards where the local children were swimming on the other side of the harbour. There were about a dozen little heads bobbing and laughing in the sea and the fishermen could see them directly in their way but they accelerated anyway in order to beach the boat on the sand. There was no shout and no warning. The excited squeals of the children changed to heartrending screams of terror and I was convinced I was going to see carnage. How they evaded the speeding vessel is a mystery. And the Afrikaner fishermen were grinning in their sport.

There really was nothing more to say. He was not going to say anything to the children and in any case they had fled in fear and he was certainly not going to give ground to me, a foreigner. He retreated sheepishly to prepare to unload his fish. His fellow sportsmen had gone to retrieve their truck and trailer with which they would collect the boat.

I was still seething but I could see that nothing was to be gained by continuing to remonstrate. Still upset, I hated them and tried to find some authority to whom I could report their cold-blooded near murder. There was nobody. Astonishingly, the incident seemed not to have troubled other holiday-makers, mainly white Namibians, swimming and sunbathing on Swakopmund leisure beach. Was this so normal, so commonplace?

The town was built by German colonialists in Victorian times and was popular largely with Namibians of German heritage though it was mainly the Afrikaners who enjoyed their sea fishing and it was them I had confronted. The behaviour of these arrogant, irresponsible and potentially murderous individuals should not, I know, be a reason or an excuse for me to hold an opinion about a whole racial group. It is untenable and wrong but having witnessed this on top of countless other displays of entitled, superior and racist conduct by some Afrikaners towards the black majority population, particularly children or people like waiters, cleaners and shop assistants, I found myself constantly checking my own prejudices.

I still hadn't recovered my equilibrium by the next morning when we were due to return home to Windhoek. Boers! I had a problem. Driving my ageing Renault Meganne hatch-back, I was probably pushing it a little when I decided to take the road over the Erongo Mountains rather than the easier route but I had done that desert journey a number of times and I fancied a change. Still upset about that frightening and unwarranted assault on the local children in the water and the disregard for safety shown by those white Afrikaner fishermen, I felt maybe that a trip through the mountains might calm me down and clear my head. I made sure we had plenty of water in the boot, loaded some bananas for the four-hour trip and did the obvious safety checks on the car, a prerequisite for any journey across remote terrain in Namibia. We would be crossing a mountain in a remote area and if we were to have a problem there would be nowhere to get help.

I was in no hurry, having all day to reach the capital. We left Swakob' and eventually reached the mountain road. My ageing Meganne was a little underpowered for these journeys but had served me well so far so I just had to accept that I would have to change down and take my time on the hills. It was when we began to climb and labour that, peering in my rearview mirror, I noticed a cloud of dust from the vehicle in the distance that appeared to be gaining on me. It was impossible to pass on these single-track gravel roads and there was nowhere to pull off. Though whatever was behind me was some way off, it was travelling at speed and would soon be closing in.

When it finally loomed in my mirror, I could see that it was a Toyota Landcruiser "backie" and that there were two young white men in the front. Boers again. In my mood I readily assumed that this was another case of entitled Afrikaners needing to assert themselves. They came far closer than was strictly necessary. It is challenging to drive on difficult climbing and twisting gravel roads while acutely aware that there is an aggressive driver constantly on your tail anxious to pass. The dust being kicked up by their backie was adding to my difficulties in seeing anything. There was little I could do and what made matters worse was that the old Renault was steadily slowing down. I worried that they might assume I was doing so on purpose but we just did not have the power. Their constant presence on my tail went on for some time and was making me irascible. Their assertiveness showed no sign of abating and my impotent frustration was growing. I just wanted them gone. I'd had enough of them and I wanted to get back to my sedate drive in the sun away from the choking dust.

I was squinting ahead intently for some way to pull off or for them to pass. When I again looked behind to check on them I noticed that our followers had disappeared. I don't know where they went. Comfort break, maybe, but they'd gone and at last we were alone on the mountain. I refocused my eyes on the road ahead and relaxed. A mile or so further on I saw some kind of obstruction. There seemed to have been an accident a short way ahead.

We were approaching a summit and there appeared to be some kind of road-block. The overheating Renault didn't need much encouragement to slow down and I cruised steadily forward until I could see an upturned flat-bed wagon silhouetted against the skyline, two of its wheels spinning slowly against the sunny morning sky. It had evidently toppled over. The horse that had been pulling it was standing alongside and many of its cloth-tied cargo bundles were strewn across the road. A young man was on the road near the cart kneeling beside another who was doubled over though thankfully there didn't seem to be any blood. Three or four of his companions standing nearby appeared to be waiting and hoping for some help. We could have driven around this blockage in the road and, though tricky, we could have ignored it if we wished. It was a remote part of a mountain road and there was no-where to get help. These young men seemed fairly desperate as they flagged us down.

I stopped the car and wound down the window as one of the lads came round to the driver's side. I expected they might need assistance to right the cart and get on their way.

"Help?" I asked. "You need help?" English is the second official language in Namibia though most of the indigenous population don't speak it.

"Food? You have food?"

We passed the bananas we had left through the window. That was all we had.

"Water? Please, water?"

I remembered that I did have a ten-litre plastic container of drinking water in the boot that I had packed for our journey. This close to home, I calculated that we could manage without it and their need seemed greater so I stepped out of the car and walked to the rear. He strutted behind as I went to open the boot. As I did so I thought how curious it was that they hadn't asked for assistance to set the cart right. It occurred to me also that there were about five able bodied young men who could do that themselves if necessary. Handing over the water, I became convinced that something wasn't right and just at the moment that I began to suspect we were in danger I heard a vehicle approaching from the rear.

Those same two young Afrikaners pulled up alongside us in their Toyota backie. The road was wider here and they could have taken the opportunity to pass us and get on their way but they didn't. They stopped beside us in the middle of the gravel road.

They said nothing but the passenger wound down his window and stared across imperiously. The Toyota waited alongside us. They could have left but they waited until I had returned to the Meganne, closed the door and locked it. Only then did they accelerate away in a cloud of dust. We followed without looking back.

It was a remote part of the mountain and there was nowhere to get help.

Macbeth on the Mountain

Night begins to fall over Addis Ababa. In the cloudless sky the pallor of the setting sun illuminates my mountain vantage whilst a thousand feet below the flickering lights of the city begin to appear. A dozen kites make wing for the last time before settling for the night in the tall eucalyptus trees that cover Entoto Mountain. They shake gently, whispering in the evening breeze. Their pungent scent fills the air. Evening prayers are being broadcast from the adjacent Orthodox Church.

All is still. I stand dressed from head to sandaled toe in pure white Ethiopian ceremonial costume and my kuta shawl protects me from the chill. I am fifty-six. I am King Duncan, King of Scotland. I wear a golden, bejewelled crown on my head and hold an Ethiopian prayer staff in my hand. My palace sits quietly in the shadows behind me as I gaze down at the city I am coming to love. The priest chants softly and the light thickens. It is an emotional and romantic moment for me as I try to embrace the character of Duncan during a pause when I am not needed in our dress rehearsal. I am free to take the sweet evening air and collect my thoughts. I must inhabit my king and be sure of his words.

This castle hath a pleasant seat. The air
Nimbly and sweetly recommends itself
Unto our gentle senses.

Thus King Duncan describes Macbeth's castle as he arrives, unaware that he is describing the place where he will die. These words, almost the last he speaks before being assassinated, are indicative of the man. He is generous of spirit and benign. He is also a poor judge of character, saying of Macbeth, by whom he is soon to be murdered, "We love him highly". Macbeth becomes a tyrant bathed in blood before being defeated by the army of Duncan's son, Malcolm. The rightful heir to the throne invites exiles home and declares a new politics.

The similarities with Ethiopia's past resonate. Emperor Haile Selassie ruled for forty-four years until 1974. His portrait adorns posters and T-shirts in the country half a century after his overthrow, illustrating the abiding affection in which he is still held by many. Nevertheless, like Duncan, he was clearly losing control towards the end. The exact nature of The Emperor's death still remains a mystery though it is said that he was smothered in bed with his own pillow wielded by Colonel Mengistu Haile Mariam who had deposed him. In 1992 the blood-soaked tyrant, Mengistu was defeated and a new government came to power led by Meles Zenawi

It is during Meles Zenawi's premiership that our play takes place. It is being performed at the former palace of Emperor Menelik II on Entoto Mountain to the north of the capital. After centuries of itinerant rule by successive monarchs, Menelik and his Empress Taitu established their royal palace here late in the nineteenth century. It commands a prominent position with excellent visibility and would have been easy to defend. It is indeed a "pleasant seat", graced with forests and fine views over the vast natural crucible in which the current capital sits. Addis Ababa (*New Flower*) was then merely a village. Owing to the mountain's chilly air and remote situation, Menelik was eventually persuaded by his Empress to relocate to Addis Ababa where there are hot springs and a hospitable climate. Their former palace still stands as a site of national importance.

Menelik's palace lacks the ostentation and refinement normally associated with a royal residence. Tucked away behind the imposing painted splendour of Entoto Maryam Orthodox Church in whose land it stands, the palace is a cluster of small curved, thatched, wattle and daub, mainly single-storey buildings. The former royal bedroom is nobler, a two-storey structure with the best country views and a substantial wooden veranda. The site is well preserved and signs adorn each of the rooms and outbuildings denoting their former uses. Incongruously, the boundary fence is made of corrugated zinc like more prosaic buildings and yards in Ethiopia. Outside the spacious main hall, the slightly raised royal terrace is the stage on which our play is to be performed. The audience is to be seated in the grassy area below. It is a privilege to be allowed to perform here.

I was made increasingly aware of the political relevance of Shakespeare's work down the ages during an embarrassing incident that occurred during our months of rehearsals. I had been asked to help out at the International Primary School. They had enjoyed a successful Shakespeare Week and with Jo, our Lady Macbeth, we were to perform the famous sleepwalking scene. I arrived before Jo and encountered an Ethiopian man of imposing stature. Animated and handsome and sporting a greying goatee beard, he was dressed in white cloak and flowing white shawl and he held an imposing sword in its scabbard.

He introduced himself to me as Abebe, a lawyer who had three children at the school and told me that he'd also been asked to help, as a parent, and was to perform a scene in Amharic from *Othello*. He mentioned that he was particularly fond of Shakespeare and that he said that there was a great tradition of Shakespeare in Ethiopia.

"Is this something you've done before then," I asked, "acting in Shakespeare plays?"

"Yes, I have done some acting in my time before I became a lawyer."

"Do you know about our *Macbeth* that we are doing in a few weeks? It will be on for three nights at Menelik's Palace on Entoto. We have been rehearsing for what seems like months."

He smiled understandingly, "Yes, I have heard it is happening and I hope to be there."

"That's great. I'm nervous but I think it should be all right. I wonder, we don't have many local people in our group so maybe you might like to join us. I must say you look every bit the part of a Shakespearean actor, dressed as Othello. We have this great Italian director called Rosanna. Could I give you her number in case you decide you would like to join?"

'You know, I might like that." He was about to say more when he saw Jo come in and he stood up courteously.

As soon as she saw us, Jo's eyes widened with shock and she ran gasping from the room. I excused myself from Abebe and went to see what the matter was.

"Don't you know who that is?" she asked, face animated with excitement.

'Yes, Abebe. He's a parent at the school. I just met him. He's a lawyer he says."

"How could you not recognise him for God's sake? That is none other than Ato Abebe Balcha. You have to take a photo of me with him. Please. I'll find my camera." She scrambled in her handbag searching.

"Abebe who?"

"Abebe Balcha is the most famous Ethiopian actor of his generation. He is huge. Been in films, starred in every Shakespeare stage production for decades. Oh my God, let's get a picture. Please. Please take my picture with him."

I was mortified and offered profuse apologies to Ato Balcha but he was modest and gracious at my embarrassment that I had failed to recognise him. He spoke to us more about some of the theatre that he had been involved in and the nature of the audience. Though he was now a lawyer, he had done it all.

"During the Derg everything was political and propaganda. Performing *Othello* in Amharic was wild. We encountered people throwing shoes at Iago or shouting or trying to advise Othello. And there was censorship. But the audience understands. There was this connection between the audience and us you know. You do some act and then all of a sudden." He smiled and paused, posing, spreading his arms and expanding his chest. "Just freeze then people will know that this part has been deleted from the script by the censors. The Ethiopian audience understands."

"But Shakespeare continued to be performed during the Derg?" I asked him, wanting to explore my theory about the similarity between Mengistu and Macbeth. "You did *Othello* but what about *Macbeth*? Were you allowed to perform it, given the content and the politics and so on?"

"At the time of the Derg, we had also prepared *Macbeth*. After the usual period of rehearsals and technical preparations, we performed the first night of what was to be a run in Addis. The following day the play was banned by order of government."

Mengistu had clearly recognised himself.

***

After months of preparation the company finally relocated to rehearse at the Palace of Emperor Menelik ll. A banquet had just occurred and the grounds were bedecked with Ethiopian flags and banners in the national colours of green, yellow and red, giving the whole complex a triumphal appearance. There is a palpable sense of ancient history in this cluster of buildings and this medieval ambience was much in evidence when we were finally able to take possession of the space and saw that the banquet had left its mark. The grassy area that was to become our auditorium was despoiled with filth; scraps of oily paper, fragments of tissue, strips of bloody meat and other half-eaten food detritus. The air, particularly in the main hall of the palace, was fetid with the stench of blood, raw meat and fermenting foodstuffs.

As we contemplated this disturbing scene, I looked for somewhere to sit. An upended log caught my eye and it seemed to be the perfect height for a stool. It was prominently placed in the centre of the grassy area and it might have seemed an ostentatious place to park myself. I was to be the king, though, and everywhere else was just filthy. As I approached my stool I was driven from it by the slivers of raw muscle tissue, sinew and drying blood that clung to it. Placed in the middle of the palace grounds in what was to become our auditorium, this was a butcher's block fit for a king.

We cleared up the mess and the pile of rubbish was burned by one of the palace guards, the acrid smoke adding to the atmosphere. Other remnants of the feast took longer to clear. The following day carcasses, blood stained goatskins and entrails were still being removed from what then became our dressing room. Even after a week, the odour of blood lingered in the room where, off-stage, my King Duncan and his nemesis, Macbeth, were both to meet their deaths.

***

Emperor Menelik's Palace sits at the top of a mountain. There is a steep road linking this remote settlement to the capital city and we are driven up. The wooded hills are important in supporting many livelihoods. When the capital city was relocated to Addis Ababa the building, cooking and heating needs of the growing population rapidly deforested the area. An ecological and human disaster was averted only by the planting of quick growing incipient eucalyptus trees and they now flourish on the hills that surround Addis Ababa providing fuel for the populace.

Our play is ready. The first night approaches but before nightfall there is the stir of human enterprise. The theatregoers ascend to the Palace.

Descending, there is a succession of women, some just teenagers, dressed in rags and bent double. They are laden more than pack mules by enormous faggots of wood. These wood carrying women are self-employed and carry their loads down to the edge of the city to sell as firewood. For this they receive a pittance.

There is a hum of activity around the Palace. The modest settlement is busy. Its dirt tracks bustle with scant herds of scraggy goats and wares and foodstuffs are spread out for sale on cloths on the dusty earth. Sensing the potential for commerce as the affluent members of the audience arrive, the villagers assemble a lively impromptu market. These same villagers are economically excluded from our play.

A princess will be there, the granddaughter of Emperor Haile Selassie. His Excellency the Ambassador to Ethiopia for Great Britain and Northern Ireland and many other members of the diplomatic corps of various foreign countries will also attend. So will our new acquaintance, the great Ato Abebe Balcha, the finest Ethiopian actor of his generation. Over the three nights the audiences will largely comprise white foreign workers of NGO's, charities or foreign businesses who can afford the entry charge. A few wealthy Ethiopians will be in attendance as well as those who have been bought tickets by members of the cast and other foreign friends. In order to watch this amateur production of Shakespeare's *Macbeth* at this august venue on the mountain, the sum of 100 Ethiopian Birr (ETB) has to be paid for a seat on a low wooden bench or 50 to stand at the rear or sit on the ground. I have bought tickets for my friend Ato Taye Makonen and his partner, Birhanne. He has always loved the plays of Shakespeare but 100 ETB is a month's rent for their tiny home so they could never afford it. The wood carrying women who climb up the mountain and haul their impossible burdens downhill for several miles receive less than 5 ETB per load. Entoto Mariam Orthodox Church, the landlord, is charging a fee of 10,000 ETB for the use of the palace. Addis Stage, our amateur theatre group, has to cover its costs. It is a matter of economics.

Shakespeare faced similar challenges and worked with small troupes of players. Thus his plays are often structured to provide opportunities for an actor to play several roles. I am no exception and in our *Macbeth,* as well as playing King Duncan, I return later as the Doctor attending Macbeth and Lady Macbeth.

In the final Act King Macbeth is losing control of his powers, both politically and mentally. He is desperate. His guilt-ridden queen has taken her own life, his lords are deserting to those seeking to depose him and he realises that his "vaulting ambition" has overreached itself and is about to cost him everything. He knows he is finished but is still defiant. As he gazes over his battlements preparing to fight to the last, he appeals to his terrified physician:

If thou couldst, doctor, cast
The water of my land, find her disease,
And purge it to a sound and pristine health...

Like Mengistu, Macbeth has murdered his king whom he should have protected. Like many despots down the centuries, in his own interest, he has betrayed his closest comrades and had them and their families killed. His deserting lords report that, "those he commands move only in command/ Nothing in love". He is a tyrant. For his own narcissistic ambition and ill-advised sense of entitlement he has destroyed everything and brought his country to ruin. He now craves to find "her disease".

The Doctor knows that the cause of the country's sickness is standing right in front of him.

Jewels and Binoculars

We have endured three nights of enjoyable but challenging trekking in the spectacular Simien Mountains National Park in northern Ethiopia. My house-mate, Ed, and two young visitors from England, Matt and Andy and I are refreshing ourselves with a beer at the L Shaped Hotel in Gonder.

We are an odd bunch. Though Ed and I are relatively acclimatised to some altitude, living at 1800 metres in Bahir Dar, Ed smokes cigarettes and small cigars and I am more than twice the age of the other two members. We had been climbing at between 3500 and 4000 metres, and for Matt and Andy, recently arrived in Ethiopia, this is a considerable disadvantage when unused to the thinner air. In addition, though he had played a little football occasionally, Andy is by his own admission, fairly out of shape. Matt is probably the fittest and strongest of us all but he had chosen to bring heavy photographic equipment which not only gave him considerably more to carry but also meant he was unable to use walking poles. So we were all handicapped on the trek in one way or another and we had tried to look out for each other and to walk at the pace of the slowest.

Ed is young enough to be my son and he never misses a chance for ageist jibe at my expense so I am not surprised by his opening to our conversation.

"In all honesty, lads, I think we really ought to congratulate David on his achievement. Not bad for a seventy-year-old." He mischievously adds more than ten years to my age.

Matt responds with, "Or Andy's seventy year old knees."

Though only twenty-seven, Andy had been told by his GP that he had the knees of a seventy year old.

"Then there's Matt's seventy year old camera," I offer because Matt had been lugging around an old-fashioned large-format camera and tripod, which only looked seventy years old though it wasn't.

We are too kind to refer to Ed's smoking habit though it isn't seventy a day.

***

The Simien Mountains National Park was designated a World Heritage Site by UNESCO in 1979. The area was formed by volcanic activity producing rock that was soft enough to have been eroded over time into spectacular escarpments, cliffs and valleys. It is not a walk for the faint-hearted or unfit. Though trekking tends to follow paths, few are on level ground and most involve long exhausting climbs or awkward descents over rocky, boulder-strewn land or thick volcanic dust. The range varies in altitude from three thousand metres to the highest peak at over four thousand five hundred.

In addition to enormous skies rarely seen elsewhere and extensive mountainous skyscapes, there is also the attraction of endemic wildlife. To be walking at high altitude and to look down to see lammergeier vultures and brown backed eagles flying hundreds of metres below is a compelling reason to make the effort. The rare Walia ibex with its huge horns, curved like scimitars, is only to be found in the Simiens and one was waiting to greet us at the entrance of our third campsite, staying around long enough to satisfy all but the slowest, most old fashioned of photographers. Widespread in the mountains but only seen here there are thousands of gelada baboons and, unlike their aggressive cousins elsewhere, they are extremely friendly; they continually dig the earth for roots with a bongo playing action or groom each other incessantly while humans can approach to within a metre of them.

One animal that is certainly not rare though it is absolutely necessary in the mountains is the mule and we would have had to have been very rugged indeed to have undertaken the trip without its assistance. In fact we'd had to enlist quite an army of assistants for the three-night trek. There are many rules to be obeyed when visiting the Simiens and one is to hire an armed scout. Some of these scouts carry Kalashnikov AK47s but our scout had only a bolt-action rifle. Their purpose was never made explicit to us though it is evidently meant for our protection from animal or human threat. We also hired a guide, as advised, as well as a chef and his assistant and the three muleteers.

A keen fan of Bob Dylan, Ed was particularly interested in the mules as he had some notion of a specific photograph that he wanted to capture which involved one dressed in some paraphernalia. But it was Andy who ended up with the mule first. The walking was exhausting but the rewards of the effort were twofold. There was the physical benefit of the exercise for its own sake. Secondly there was the breathtaking landscape that can only be viewed if reached on foot. Nevertheless, after our first full day of around 15 kilometres the last section of which was a long steep haul uphill through thick black ankle-deep volcanic dust and over boulders, we were totally and utterly spent. Three of us recovered fairly quickly, though, and with a break for a cold shower and a coffee, we hiked a little trek of a kilometre or so up to a peak close to Gich camp to see sunset over the mountains. Not Andy, who declared that he was broken. I wanted to cheer him up and to remind him that he was privileged to be experiencing this extra special journey in a country that would be visited by few people he would ever know in his life.

"On a scale of ten, Andy, how happy are you right now?"

"Five!" He didn't take long to consider; he knew how he was feeling.

At one point during the next day, he somehow guessed that I was going to ask him again and he warned me off saying the score was likely to be much lower. We had been warned that that day was going to be an even longer and harder walk. He wasn't sure he was going to be able to succeed even with the walking pole he had eventually and reluctantly agreed to borrow from me. We decided to hire an extra mule to accompany us in case Andy felt the need for some assistance. He coped well with the first part of the walk including some arduous climbs but our guide had warned us that we faced a really difficult two-hour climb before lunch. Indeed it was tough; we were steadily ascending from 3600 metres to the highest point we reached at 4070 metres. Half way into this walk, the mule's day became suddenly harder as Andy decided that the time had come for a ride.

It was then that I remembered the tale Noveed had told me about when he had had to resort to the mule. My fellow volunteer, Noveed, a gay young Brummie, would be the first to admit that he was no tough outdoorsman and, like Andy, when he had trekked the Simiens previously, he had had to rely on the mule. His extra problem though was that as he was well over six feet tall he had the added difficulty of his feet dragging on the ground. With his wild Afro hair and dangling legs, it conjured quite a picture which took my mind off the ordeal for a while.

We were all finding it tough and we had devised a strategem that helped us. I presume that it was because I was the oldest that I found myself at the front placing one foot agonisingly slowly in front of the other and repeatedly calling to Getachaw, the guide, to slow down. In this fashion, we made it to the 4070 metre summit though when approaching 4000 metres the air seemed so thin as to be almost impossible to breathe and both of the two younger lads, unused to altitude, experienced temporary headaches.

While Andy was on the mule, which we had named Muffin, Ed said he fancied a turn himself. He swore that it was only for the experience and not because he was struggling particularly with the difficulty of the climb. I didn't believe him.

"There is a price, Ed, if you ride that mule and I don't," I told him.

"What kind of price?"

"If you get on that mule and I continue to walk, you have to refrain from ever again using ageist comments to me or about me."

Ed decided to carry on walking. He wasn't letting me off that easily.

It was as we approached the peak, that he decided the time was right for the business with the mule so we asked the guides to stop for a water break. Setting up the mule shoot with the animal in regalia took some doing. While the others rested, Ed and I approached the mule but we both backed off as it turned suspiciously and stepped towards us. We enlisted the assistance of one of the muleteers to prepare his charge as we weren't sure how to proceed with the negotiation. Without shared language between us and the mule-man, not to mention the animal, this was a difficult process and we somehow gestured to him that we needed the mule to stand still while Ed dangled things on its head. He had surely never had such a request like this before but, perplexed, he soothed the animal, speaking gently to it and managed to persuade it to stand still and allow us to approach. Ed was well prepared. He had asked to borrow my binoculars and he produced a rudimentary necklace that he had previously fashioned from string and silver balls made from rolled tin-foil. Fortunately, Dylan's song specifies that these things hang from the head of a mule. Trying to hang them around the neck would have been a step too far. Thus, Ed managed to hang the binoculars on one ear of the mule and the necklace on the other and the beast posed long enough for him to get his photograph of "jewels and binoculars hanging from the head of a mule". We were not worried when it stepped away with the tin-foil necklace though I had to ask the mule keeper to chase it to retrieve my binoculars. So Ed got his photograph though he never told me what he intended to do with it. It was difficult to offer an explanation in response to the looks of astonishment on Ethiopian faces on seeing this performance.

At the top of our mountain, I sang a poem and the mule went home. All the way up, through the ever thinning air, as I placed one foot after another, I was singing under my breath the poem I once saw performed live by Ivor Cutler, the late eccentric Scottish poet. At some point after we had reached the apex, I treated the party to a rendition, chanted in a very slow Scottish drawl:

"Put your best foot forward
but don't forget the other one;
don't forget the other one as well."

The mule went home because he had done his job and that was the rule. Another rule threatened to mar our second full day's walk and it was Matt who was the transgressor. In addition to the armed scouts who were hired to accompany walkers there were numerous similarly armed but more intimidating National Park Guards who wore camouflage fatigues and looked very militaristic. It was one of these rather stern guards who had spotted Matt's tripod and assumed he was a professional photographer with what looked like a large video or cine camera. It was against the rules to use a large camera without a permit which should have been purchased at the entrance to the park and which could not be had retrospectively. The guard instructed Getachaw to tell Matt not to use that camera. Matt was carrying and intending to use a professional quality large-format camera so it was, indeed, a hefty piece of equipment but we all tried to explain that it was not video and it was not for commercial purposes; that Matt was essentially a hobby photographer. There was no budging the guard and, even after he had departed in another direction, Getachaw said he feared for his job if he allowed Matt any further use of this particular apparatus.

At the end of the walk that day we met the National Park manager in the "community centre", a green painted, mud walled building with corrugated zinc roof across the road from the camp-site at Chennek. We explained the situation to him and received his permission to use the equipment. Though Matt had missed some wonderful shots that day, he did manage for the rest of the trip, in his words, "to make some pictures". This community centre served cold bottled beer and we were certainly ready for a few before crossing the road to the camp for our last evening.

***

As night falls, so does the rain and it becomes seriously cold. We are dressed in every available layer and we are going to have to endure a freezing night under canvas. First, though, after a simple hot meal we huddle together in a circular roofed shelter around a hastily made camp-fire. The long logs radiate from the centre of the heat, each one being pushed toward the flames as it burns down. We are twelve in number; we four, our hired help, cooks, guards and armed men. Shoulder to shoulder, we sit warmly, intermittently staring at the fire and at each other. Although there is a campfire I am too exhausted to sing.

We share the whisky we had brought along for the trip with those of our Ethiopian company who would accept it and, with very little common language, we spend a few hours together in the dark watching Bushman's TV. Vivid Ethiopian eyes reflect the fire, which also glints on the magazines of the AK 47s being held perilously close to the heat.

Did You Say Something?

Sorry, Mum, did you say something? I haven't been listening I'm afraid.

We're in your room in the care home. Sometimes though, occasionally, you are confused as to where you are supposed to be. That seemingly impenetrable fog leaves you lost. You rarely seem alarmed – just vacantly questioning. Now in your tenth decade you still have the looks; your wavy hair retains some of its dark colour, your nails are well manicured and, though confined to your wheelchair, you still preserve some of your vanity that has always been there.

It is a clean first floor room with a decent view over the suburbs. Family photographs adorn the walls and in pride of place, professionally framed, hang Dad's medals as well as the photograph of him in his Royal Navy uniform. There is a story behind each of these medals; each one is a reward for service and bravery. I've asked for you to be in your wheelchair so I can bring you here for some privacy. It is insufferably hot and airless but you do not seem to notice. Here we can talk together and see what we can delve from your past. I am reading to you from your own memoirs. Written in biro in neat block capitals to begin with, these are notes from a life; from your life, started some thirty or more years ago before the mist of old age descended and left you lost. The lined paper is yellowed now and dog-eared. The simple prose is lacking in imagery but the life described pulses with a fiery heartbeat.

We have read of your early years, of your Salvation Army parents and their many siblings. You wrote of the poverty endured and *"THE BEGINNING OF THE DEPRESSION, WHEN MEN MARCHED FROM THE NORTH EAST DOWN TO LONDON TO PROTEST."* The Jarrow March from 1936. You were only seven and yet it is part of your story. We have read of your various temporary homes where you had to live while your metal turner father had to take any kind of work he could find. You tell of how he would cut cardboard each day to line your worn shoes before you were sent to school. Some of the names, Vessey Road, Carlton or Trent Street, Worksop elicit a flicker of recognition though mostly you remain mystified.

My reading is brusquely interrupted at one point when you comment on the folder of papers in my hand.

"It must have taken you ages to write all this much," You say, peering into my eyes, love and admiration in your voice. "How did you remember all that?" You seem proud of me for your achievement.

'Mum, it's your work," I try to explain. "You wrote it. It's what you remember of your life."

Quietly, modestly, in diligent prose, you set down your life; the author in space; too late to appreciate; too late to celebrate. These found faded pages tell an enormous story, read by no one because you told no one. I ache to hear you tell me more of what you have seen, what you have done, what was done to you and what you have written about. I ache. My heart aches. These eloquent words you speak to me and it is too late to say, "Sorry, Mum, did you say something? I haven't been listening, I'm afraid."

The reading continues and you seem, whilst not closely familiar with these events from your childhood, at least comforted. My reading to you seems to make you happy and I am gratified at least to have this tool to try to reach back into the person you were; the person you still are. So we continue. You are ten by this time.

"THOSE WERE DAYS WHEN CHILDREN COULD HAPPILY PLAY OUT ON THE STREETS FOR HOURS WITH NO WORRIES. THERE WERE SOME OUTBUILDINGS AT THE BACK OF THE SHOP WHERE WE LET OUR IMAGINATIONS GO MAD. WE MADE HOUSES, SHOPS, CARS AND PLAYED INNOCENTLY FOR HOURS. WE WERE PLAYING THERE ON SUNDAY MORNING THE 3RD SEPTEMBER 1939 WHEN A BOY CAME RUNNING....."

Again you speak, interrupting me before I can complete your sentence.

"War!" you say. A distinct glimmer in the dense fog. "It's the war starting."

You can't remember your own 90th birthday party with all the family four years ago. You struggle to know the names of your dozen grandchildren or your great grandchildren. You can't tell me what you ate for lunch and you have forgotten that you are unable to stand unaided. And yet the mention of that fateful day cuts like a searchlight through the night.

War! You are yet to meet him but the boy with whom you will spend sixty years of your life and with whom you will come to have four children is just fifteen and already serving in a warship, HMS Ark Royal. He is already at war.

We read on now. After nearly an hour I attempt to have a rest to save my voice but you insist that I continue.

My granddad now is engaged in war work at a shipyard, helping the war effort and he can only come home at weekends. You and your three young siblings have moved back home to Sunderland. Your mum, my Nana, can't cope without him so at thirteen you become the housekeeper, *"THE LITTLE DRUDGE"*. As the centre couldn't hold, you prevented things from falling apart. Nana did help you with the laundry though. It was such heavy work. Everything went into a big tub and was beaten with a large stick called a poss. When I stumble over the unfamiliar word, *"POSS"*, you explain it to me, another spark in the dark.

Later we will read of your accounts of a life of service to others, particularly to the men, including your husband and sons who expected so much. We will read of your endless struggle to protect and provide for those you love, often through hardship.

Nowhere in your story, though will we encounter heroics or derring do. Your life is one where you listen to the exploits of others. You do not drunkenly hold the room, a raconteur, with tales of medal winning bravery, drunken fights or loveless childhood struggles. Though your story is one of facilitating the lives of others, these things belong in a different tale. His story.

My throat is dry and I must end our shared reading. I close your book for now, saying, "This is your life," and I smile but the reference to Eamonn Andrews is lost on you. This is your life: you wrote it; you lived it. We will read some more next time.

Downstairs, with a kiss goodbye, I leave you in the lounge. As I am showing your folded pages to one of the care staff and explaining proudly how you have written your life story and we have been sharing it, she is impressed. I glance toward you over her shoulder for a last goodbye smile and a blown kiss and I discern a new knowing expression on your face. Your fleeting smile shows a glint in your eyes and a satisfied pride and this time, for once, I feel that it is you who is the object of this pride, not me.

The Power of Song

Almost sixty years ago on a midsummer morning in rural Warwickshire, warmed by a hazy sunshine, standing near the cellar door of a remote country inn, brow sweating gently from labour and the sun's warmth, I stand, a teenage "drayman". I am halted in my tracks, a crate of empty beer bottles in my hands, by the faint but haunting unaccompanied solo soprano melody I can hear from a distance. I scour the surrounding countryside and locate the sound, its source a young woman, oblivious to any audience, strolling alone across a field in the nearby valley way below the level of the road on which I am standing. She appears minute as she wanders in her musical walk several hundred yards away, the mid morning haze almost obscuring this vision of a country idyll though the folk song can be heard above the rustling of grasses and the wind in the trees.

***

Forty years ago the peace of a relaxing early Sunday sunny morning swim while holidaying beside the Aegean sea is broken by the heartfelt high pitched discordant keening of a disembodied voice sung at full volume by the unknown Greek woman as she swims sedately, oblivious to any audience, away from the shore in a straight line, conscious of nothing but her communion with her god. It is Sunday and it thus becomes clear that this is a hymn, possibly in the Greek Orthodox tradition. The regular hushing, murmuring wash of the marble-glittering waves on the warming sand provides the only musical accompaniment.

***

On either side the fluted columns of the cathedral walls and the high gothic windows soar into the vast vaulted space. Before the looming brass organ pipes and the high altar in

Exeter Cathedral stand the three female singers of Nova Koliada. It is winter outside, late January and the substantial audience is dressed to stay warm. The concert is held both to raise funds for the suffering people of Ukraine and to bring hope and to warm the hearts of those whose emotions are torn to shreds as a result of Russia's invasion and occupation of the East of their country. Many of those traumatised souls are here. Some have families and friends who are trapped in the conflict.

Each of the three unaccompanied singers, dressed full length in plain crimson dresses, wears two white crepe flowers in her hair. One carries in her hand a small leafless bush about a metre in length with three or four branches. *Koliada* is the ancient Slav tradition of late winter song rituals celebrating renewal of light and life - of hope.

The first song begins with an alto voice providing a ground, unexpectedly low pitched for a female voice. This is overlaid by melodies which fill the vast void above. Now a keening wail adds the vertical to the erstwhile horizontal as the harmonic whole becomes so dense as to press the heart, palpably filling emptiness. With the volume of this ululating prayer and the fulsome commitment from just three unaccompanied voices, I am transported.

***

Approaching mid-day now in the maize field and though the corn stands more than head height there is no shade and it would have been a good idea to have worn a hat as it is getting hotter. I wish I had some water to slake my dry throat as I make my way with the men along the path through the maize towards the collective farm clubhouse for the wedding feast. The dried earth path, one or two metres wide, which leads diagonally from corner to corner of the field has been worn by the repeated footsteps of villagers walking to the single small shop or to the varicoloured, randomly tiled bus shelter on the main road. Alongside the road to town stands an avenue of mature birch trees and their sussuration in a gentle breeze can be heard continually as can the subdued late morning birdsong.

Above the corn, the vast azure sky is a vaulted heaven. The drying maize is almost ready now for harvesting, as are the head high sunflowers in the nearby fields of this collective farm. These small fields lie between the homesteads with their kitchen gardens and the communal buildings and *kolhoz* (collective farm) of tiny Chemodanivka, in Sumy Oblast, not too far from the border with Russia. Beyond lie the vast flat fields in which wheat and other cereals for the Soviet population are grown.

I am caught off guard when suddenly the song starts, unaccompanied by instruments, though none of the locals of the collective would be surprised because this is strongly traditional on any occasion where friends and family gather. It is said of Ukraine that folksong is the soul of the people.

It begins with the men singing in unison in several registers. The bass voices resonate with such power as almost to shake the corn. Above them, lighter and airier, the sound of tenor voices soars towards the heavens. The space between is filled with strong baritones. The men step happily towards the venue, the summer air full of the male voice choir, the rhythm of the song in time with our walking.

A shocking shriek pierces the sky; a keening, scarcely tuneful ululation, rides above the men's voices, soaring over their song. It seems barely sustainable until the sound is joined by other women's voices, altos and contraltos; voices which give warmth and depth to the rest of the choir. The women are dressed in traditional national costume and are walking in a group behind the men. They have, as in the days of their ancestors, picked up on the musical cues from the men and, as in so many other ways, they take the lead. The women's voices seem even more powerful than those of their men. These unaccompanied harmonies in at least six registers meld into a rich and warming soundtrack to an ebullient walk through the *kukurusi* to the wedding.

Ivan Eufimovich, my father-in-law, is with me on our musical walk through the corn to the wedding in the village collective, joining in heartily with his fearless voice.

He once lamented that traditional song in Ukraine had been suppressed from early Soviet times as part of russification in order to remove the strong national pride of its people and that some became afraid to be heard singing, to be enjoying the soul of the nation. He had no fear and on many occasions during Soviet times in the village where he had lived, I enjoyed his full-throated unaccompanied bass baritone voice as he sang traditional folk songs wildly and happily with his brothers and other male friends and family under the apple trees in the yard after meals. Still today, forty-five years later I see vividly in my mind's eye, their smiling faces raised to the sky, eyes half closed in concentration and dappled with shade from the leaves of the tree as they celebrate life with song.

***

Nova Koliada are nearing the close of the concert in Exeter Cathedral. The *Koliada* festival traditionally includes an element of musical walk, often to neighbouring houses, and this concert also includes a walk in the final song.

The crimson-clad singers leave the small dais in front of the altar and approach the aisle. Faces raised to the heavens, eyes half-closed in supplication, they pass the intricately carved stone lectern and proceed along the granite aisle, worn smooth by generations of worshipers. Still singing in harmony they pass between the two sides of the audience following the tree which is borne as a standard. At one point, with a barely perceptible hand gesture from the group leader, those present are invited to hum along and this support grows soulfully, powerful in its moment of solidarity. This audience is now a congregation as the song assumes the tone of prayer in the Orthodox tradition. The tempo is that of a psalm and the combination of the mournful higher register, accompanied by the occasional tinkle of a hand bell, evokes a sense of profound loss.

Koliada is a celebration of light and hope and we have come in our hundreds to wish these things and more for the people of Ukraine and to hope also for ourselves; to take joy in the approach of spring, of rebirth, of life, of peace.

During the course of the performance, scarcely noticed, one by one, the flowers in the singers' hair have been transferred to the tree. The bare winter plant has been transformed into a spring blossom.

The Piano

The piano was heavy and had seen better days. The dark polished wood was old fashioned and battered. Not even its owner thought it a handsome piece of furniture. Originally a good quality cross-strung instrument, it now gathered dust, occasionally emitting a musty smell like that of the vestry in a country church. The piano tuner had not been for several years and on his last visit he had judged that it would now be difficult to continue to tune it very accurately. It might serve for a child to learn on, he had said.

But she loved it and as she placed her ageing hands on the familiar keys, in all her being she felt her childhood. This was the instrument on which she had learned as a little girl, the instrument on which she had been taught the Ukrainian folk songs that were so close to her heart and which she could not for a second bring herself to accept that she might no longer play. On this piano she accompanied her late father when he sang those same songs. It was the instrument she took with her when her daughters needed to learn. Apart from then, the upright piano had dominated this small living room for the best part of fifty-five years.

For some years, however, its presence had been controversial and this was heightened in view of the recent makeover. The lounge in the 1930s semi had been recently redecorated in an attempt to bring it more up to date and an ongoing dispute had peaked as to whether the clearly aged and somewhat battered piano had any place in a contemporary lounge with limited space.

Considerable effort had been made to make the room seem less dated; white walls with midnight blue either side of the chimney-breast and the once marble hearth now also painted white. Original art works, mostly from various parts of Africa, hung tastefully on the walls. Skirting boards and picture rails, though retained along with the oak mantelpiece to preserve the period integrity of the house had been stripped to bare wood. It was the maroon carpet that almost spoiled the attempt at contemporaneity. It was a top quality Wilton, The blood colour just about worked as a contrast with the pacific blue of the newly re-upholstered three-piece suite but some felt it was still rather old fashioned.

In order to make the most of the limited space, one chair was in the bay window and the sofa against the opposite wall. The other was set back beside the piano where its occupant's head would be very close to the end of the keyboard casing.

The old man sat there inches away from it, another whisky in hand, still slightly irritated about the piano's continued presence in his life. Whenever he walked into the room and saw it his hands felt like clenched fists, useless, not through anger or aggression but because of his inability to play. After seemingly endless equivocation about it he had finally come to accept that it was staying and it had all become a bit of a joke. The piano was important to his wife for many reasons, mostly sentimental and though he considered it ugly and thought its black chipped varnish and very size sucked the light out of the room that he had tried so hard to brighten, he had come to realise that it really wasn't worth continually fighting over.

"It's not a hill I am prepared to die on," he repeatedly joked.

Her old school friend, Lula, once a great advocate for the piano's right to stay, had of late begun to tease her friend about the need to part company with it. She had hosted Lula's seventieth birthday dinner. Her husband was the last one up and was rather preoccupied. Though he had had more than his usual amount to drink, he couldn't settle to go to bed. It was so dominating in the room, that ugly piano. He envisaged the space that might be available in a reorganised room if it weren't for his dark companion. The keyboard lid was as usual left open and the keys, uneven with age and use, seemed to sneer at him with a bucked tooth sardonic grin.

Which one of them would go first, he mused. He had begun, in his seventies to contemplate mortality. He was beginning to feel his age and though generally fit, his left foot occasionally gave way a little too often for his liking. The piano had been his wife's companion for a lot longer than he had; would it even now outlast him? Ironic, he thought. Though accepting defeat, he was not overly gracious. Brooding, he swallowed some more whisky.

***

The piano had always been clearly visible from the street to any passer-by who chose to glance towards the house. And, significantly, people did. On one occasion a note had been posted through the letterbox. It was from Doctor Elizabeth from Yorkshire, once another old school friend and a frequent visitor to the area to visit her brother. For some time Elizabeth had noted the piano's absence and assumed that the family had moved and taken it with them. She noticed when it had returned, however, and was delighted that her old friend had come back to live in the house of her childhood. The note re-established a friendship that had lain dormant for decades. On a subsequent visit to the house Liz urged her never to part with the instrument, not least because it had reunited them.

Jane too, yet another lifelong school-friend, had grown to love the piano. Her own mother was an accomplished pianist and she had played it on a visit to the house and commented on its fine tone. Lula also had been a keen advocate. Both had been regular young visitors when the piano occupied pride of place in her parents' front room. They loved the house, loved her parents, loved the room and loved the piano. They frequently urged her to keep it. The old man, outnumbered, knew that he had little chance of seeing the piano off but he kept up the effort, sometimes with humour and sometimes with reasoned argument. He offered to buy a new, smaller and more modern instrument. He even threatened to start playing scales. She just couldn't part with it though, frequently citing the sentimental value, the lovely tonal quality and the fact that all her friends said she should always keep it.

"You've got your father's stubbornness," he remarked in defeat.

Then she changed her mind. On reflection, she did not practise enough and her ability was rusty. She did not play frequently enough to justify buying another piano and she had to accept the fact that this piano was ageing and its quality diminishing. It wasn't very pretty and it did take up too much room. It was time to part with it. He did not feel triumphant at this volte-face because in his heart he understood what it meant to his wife. He was pleased though and he found a local family who were more than willing to take the piano at no charge for the daughter to learn on. All was arranged.

Then she changed her mind. As the time came, she just could not bear to let go of this essential part of her life. The hole it would leave in her heart was bigger than the space in the front room where it had presided for so many years. She started to play a little more though always alone and never to entertain. Her repertoire was fairly narrow, consisting mainly of snatches of those Ukrainian songs that she loved so much to play even while they broke her heart with nostalgia. She always waited for her husband to be out of the house before playing but on one occasion she did not hear him return from working in the garden. As he came through the rear door he heard her playing *Ridna Mati Moya* (*My Dear Mother*). Deeply affected, he stopped silently in his tracks, breathing quietly and standing stock-still in order to give her no excuse to stop. It was a deeply melancholic tune evocative of Ukraine, one she had played frequently in the years after they had been married. She was also singing quietly, accompanying herself, a special moment of soulful solo tranquillity. As he silently wiped away a tear, he understood why she had to keep the piano. This was the moment that he accepted that this was not a battle he would fight. This was no "hill to die on".

Then she changed her mind. A great deal of thought, discussion and calculation had gone into the anticipated redecorating of the lounge. When she had lived there with her parents, the dark piano blended in, was in synch with the old fashioned décor. Not now though. He continued to argue that it was an eyesore and she was beginning to come round to the idea that it would not really fit with what would be a new look. In addition, she was becoming aware of the development of cataracts in her right eye and arthritis in her hands all of which were beginning to impact on her ability to play. Perhaps a modern piano might be a fair compromise. In the meantime, the old man, still strong enough, single-handedly heaved the piano, one end at a time into the centre of the room and set about the decorating. They had agreed that he could get the job done, replace everything, see how it all looked and then decide. Four or five days later, the redecoration complete, the piano was returned to its eternal position.

Then she changed her mind. With the door opened wide against the wall and the chair tucked back alongside the piano there was sufficient room. It seemed an unnecessary expense to think of spending money on another used piano when this one served its purpose. When the time came to change the carpet in a few years the piano would have to be removed from the room so perhaps that was the time to think about getting rid of it. Meanwhile, the lounge being more welcoming, she found herself enjoying playing more often than before. The piano's reprieve was complete.

***

So here he was, after the dinner party, enjoying a quiet moment with another glass of his favourite Laphroaig. For a small group, the party with Lula's old school friends had been a little lively. Though mostly aged around seventy, they had never lost their love of dancing to Tamla and soul music. But now it was quiet. The few who were staying over had gone to bed and the others had left for home. Before the dancing, there had been much reminiscing. There had been eight guests and all of them lovingly remembered her parents as they had visited the house when they were teenagers. They each remembered the front room as it was and inevitably conversation centred towards the piano. Lula continued her light-hearted goading of her friend and hostess to get rid of it while Jane appealed vehemently for it to be spared. Feeling the effects of too much wine and whisky, he was just exasperated. He had given up. This was not a battle he was going to fight, or win. He was tired of it; tired of the equivocation.

So, though accepting defeat, he was not overly gracious; grumpy in fact. He sat there beside his nemesis and realised that his glass was empty. He needed to go to the kitchen for a refill. He was sleepy now and he knew he should be going to bed but he was feeling moody, melancholic, on a roll and he wanted another drink so he braced to haul himself out of the chair.

Two things happened to him simultaneously. His left hand slipped unsteadily from the arm of the chair while his unreliable left foot crumpled painfully under him. Wincing, he rotated to his left and, gritting his teeth in pain, he tried to steady himself by slamming down on the piano. Just as his clenched right fist hit the keyboard, his head struck the edge of the casing and the loud ugly bass chord was the last sound he heard. He crumpled to the floor in a heap beneath the piano keyboard and, beside the pedals, his gashed right temple soaked blood into the fine quality maroon Wilton carpet.

ACKNOWLEDGEMENTS

So many friends and family members have been subjected to these tales as they have emerged and all have offered support and encouragement. Thank you for being kind and honest.

In particular I am hugely indebted to Martin Phillips, my principal and honorary editor and critical friend who believed in me and kept me going in moments of exasperation. Without Martin's endless patience and huge input these tales would have been so much longer and far less engaging.

Thanks go also to the following for time spent reading as well as support, encouragement and ideas for improvement:

Jack and Alice Bracher who were the first to hear the first story, Nadia obviously, Nina and Steve Nicholson, Larissa Bracher, Dilys Hartley, Tim Arnold, Jane Gray, Lula Rendall, Ed Howarth, Mike Sanders, Steven Shipko, Yvette Boucher, Shimeles Lemma and Taye Makonen who always believed in me as a writer.

I acknowledge too a huge debt to those no longer with us but who taught us so much: Lilian and Hugh Roberts, Ivan Euphimovich and Stella Danilenko, Maria Yusopovna Koval and others.

They live on in these pages.

Lyrics from "Step It Out Lively" are quoted with kind permission from the Estate of Ivor Cutler.

Permission has been sought from
Umpg licensing for the words of B B King from "Born Again Human"
Vintage/ Penguin for the epigraph from "There There" by Tommy Orange
Sony Music for words from "Visions of Johanna" by Bob Dylan

Thanks also to David Morrison and team from PublishNation